STAR COMPASS

A VICTORIA ETERNAL NOVEL

ANTHEA SHARP

FIDDLEHEAD PRESS

A Victoria Eternal Novel

ANTHEA SHARP

Oliver Twist meets Firefly in this Steampunk tale of an orphan destined for the stars.

Enter a fantastical world filled with alien spacecraft and Victorian sensibilities, ball gowns and travel to the stars - where Diana Smythe, a mathematically gifted pickpocket, makes the journey from the gutter to the galaxy…

PROLOGUE

DIANA SMYTHE STARED OUT THE WINDOW OF THE FAMILY carriage and thumped the back of her heels against the leather seat, timing the beats to alternate with the clop of the horses' hooves. She didn't want to go visit the Duchess of Penderly, even if the old lady was Papa's great-aunt or somesuch. She'd much rather stay home and play with her new puppy.

The puppy was small, but Nanny told her he was going to grow into a big dog, so Diana had named him Jupiter, after the largest planet. Maybe he'd even be big enough for her to ride on. And once he was grown, maybe he could even be modded with wings, and they could fly off on adventures together up into the stars.

As the carriage rolled through the streets of London, Diana kept boredom away by watching the horse-drawn cabs and steam-powered vehicles, calculating their speeds and trajectories in her mind. Pedestrians eddied along the sidewalks, and she added them in, too, plus the random dartings of pigeons over the rooftops.

It was a lively scene, full of lines of movement and parabolic arcs she could almost see drawn across the air. Every sudden stop or acceleration changed the dynamics, and she tried to make predictions. Would the hansom cab or the omnibus reach the crossing first? Would a bird dart to the near side of the street, or the far one? Would that lady with a parasol pass the nurse pushing a pram by the time they reached the apothecary shop?

Whenever she spoke about such things, she was either patted on the head or called a very odd little girl. Only once had anyone looked at her like she made sense, and that had been Uncle Xavier. Last year, when she was only seven, he'd insisted on a maths tutor for Diana, although she was the youngest and her older siblings had no such thing.

Papa had sighed and shook his head, but within a week a tutor had arrived. Mr. Tamms had proclaimed himself astonished at her mathematical talent, and soon enough Diana was learning trigonometry and was allowed to do as many sums as she pleased.

Not today, though. After breakfast, Nanny had dressed her in her new frock, the one with the shiny buttons, and told her she was going on an important visit. Diana, engrossed with counting the facets on the crystalline buttons, had scarcely listened, even as Nanny bundled her, along with her brother and sister, into the carriage.

"Here's a sweet." Nanny had slipped a horehound candy into Diana's hand. "Now behave, young miss, and when you come home you'll be able to tumble about with Jupiter to your heart's content."

Diana knew better than to complain, so she'd taken the

candy and settled on the far end of the seat. Peter and Claudia squished in next to her, and in a few moments Mama and Papa entered the carriage and sat opposite their children. Diana peeked at them from beneath the brim of her hat.

In truth, she was a little afraid of the elegant, distant creatures who were her parents. She did not see much of Mama, and even less of Papa, although she supposed that would change as she grew up. Claudia had just turned ten, and was deemed old enough to begin taking her meals in the formal dining room with their parents, as Peter had done for the past two years. Diana felt a bit abandoned in the nursery with only Nanny for company during supper.

But there were always her old friends, the numbers and the trajectories. Nanny didn't know why Diana liked to roll her balls back and forth in the playroom, calculating when to push a smaller one out in order to collide with, or avoid, the others. But Mr. Tamms understood.

Best of all, she now had Jupiter—a constant lesson in speed and motion. Plus he covered her in sloppy puppy kisses and slept at the foot of her bed.

"Are you certain the duchess will aid us?" Mama turned to Papa, a note of concern in her sweet voice. "She is such a distant relative, after all…"

"Don't fret, my darling. Once she sees the children, and understands our predicament, I'm certain everything will turn out for the best."

Diana hardly listened to her parents. Most of her attention was taken up by watching the thick plume of steam trailing from a large omnibus clattering down the street toward them. Her parents would never dream of taking public transport about London. That was for the working class, not nobility like themselves.

Still, it looked like great fun to ride about so quickly in a vehicle powered by steam and gears. The omnibus was going at quite a clip; certainly faster than Jupiter could run.

Diana undid the latches and lowered the window a bit, leaning out slightly so she could taste the air as the omnibus swept past.

Something was wrong, though. The lines of travel weren't parallel. For a moment her lungs squeezed so tight she could barely breathe. It was like watching two of her balls meant to zip past one another instead wobble into a collision course.

"Mama?" she asked in a small voice.

"But what about the debts?" Mama did not hear her, and continued speaking to Papa. "Do you truly think she will agree to cover them?"

"Mama!" Diana tried again.

"Now, Diana dear, no need to shout—"

Mama's words were obliterated by the blast of the omnibus's horn.

It was coming too fast.

Too close.

There was a horrible crunch and the carriage spun sickeningly about. Diana screamed as they turned and tilted. She felt herself slipping out the window, and tried to grab on to something—*anything*—but her scrabbling fingers could find no purchase.

"Diana!" Papa bellowed as she was flung out of the coach.

She tried to tuck her head down, to make herself into a

little ball so she would not break her arm the way she had when she'd fallen out of the apple tree last summer. The air was full of the screech of metal, and people screaming.

Then a bigger crash, that sounded like the sky was breaking. A flash of light and heat, and a *whump* that vibrated through Diana's chest.

Her head collided with something, and everything went away into the black.

CHAPTER 1

8 YEARS LATER

THE PICKPOCKET KNOWN AS DIVER SLIPPED THROUGH THE throngs at the Southampton docks, her nimble fingers dipping into a pocket here, a reticule there. The pattern of working a crowd had become as simple to her as breathing, the trajectories predictable, and she used them to her advantage.

She knew when a space would open up for her to pass through, how to avoid becoming trapped in a knot of people, the way the rich nobs strolled leisurely along without much change in direction, as though they owned the very air. She never lingered too long in one place, and usually only lifted small items: a shilling, a kerchief, a thimble. Things that could be misplaced just as easily as stolen.

She was fast enough to make up for it, though, and her slight pickings grew until she judged that her own well-hidden purse was heavy enough.

Then, with a smile for the gentleman whom she'd just relieved of some coin, and a twirl of her battered parasol, she left the docks. Better to depart now, before raising any suspicions. There was a new policeman on patrol, and she didn't want to run afoul of the fellow. Word was he hadn't yet been bribed by the gang runners to look the other way.

Diana wasn't one of the gang rats, though it cost her a fair bit of her weekly take to maintain her independence. Sometimes she wondered if it was worth it—but then she remembered those first, horrible months on the London streets. And the orphanage before that…

With a clang, she slammed the door on those thoughts. Her past was gone. There was only the present, and the life she'd scraped up for herself. Her independence was one of the most valuable things she had, and bedamned if she would give it up lightly.

She ducked down a nearby alley to transform herself. Off went her skirt and matching jacket, revealing the trousers and work shirt beneath. She traded her bonnet for a plain cap, stuffing her hair beneath the stained wool. Finally, she turned her skirt and jacket inside out and wrapped them around the parasol to make a nondescript bundle.

With a grimace, she scraped some muck from a nearby puddle and smudged her face, especially around the jaw. Best to give the impression she was a boy—she'd learned that lesson some time ago. Diana, the girl who'd grown up in an elegant house in Mayfair, was gone forever, changed to Diver, a scrappy lad from the stews of London.

It was getting harder to pass as a boy, though, as she

grew older. She'd lost track of her birthdays in those first, dreadful years after the accident. Now she figured she was sixteen or thereabouts. Maybe seventeen. Living on the streets had delayed her growth—but not halted it altogether.

It used to be a fine disguise, to dress in the castoffs of some noble girl while she worked the crowd. Now, though, she was the recipient of lingering glances she didn't much like, and leering smiles that made her queasy. She knew where that led, and that was a path she refused to take. She'd seen girls her own age used up in only a few years, and nothing to show for it.

Maybe 'twas time to hack off her hair, but she shied away from the thought. Shearing it off felt like losing an essential part of herself and giving in completely to the harshness of the streets. Leastwise, that's what she told herself. It tasted better in her mouth than the notion she was vain about her curling, toffee-colored tresses.

And if worst came to worst, she might need her pretty hair—if she ever grew so desperate as to take the path of those other girls.

Overhead, the roar of a ship taking off from the space-port distracted her from her grim thoughts. A hauler, from the sound of the engines, loaded with cargo and headed out-system.

Diana tilted her head. The ship should be visible between the buildings in just a moment… *there*. Heavy-bodied and powerful, a mid-century Frauke, probably bound for one of the colonies out along the spiral arm.

She watched until it was just a speck in the sky, trying

not to think of the stars shining behind the blue. Trying not to think of what it would mean to save enough to book passage out to a new planet, where she could start over. Where her life wouldn't be a constant scrabble, always looking over her shoulder for trouble.

Every streetrat had that dream, to board a ship headed to the stars. It was as impossible as the storyvid tales of fortunes suddenly regained, of lost families reappearing to fold missing orphans back into their arms. But her life was not a storyvid. She knew well enough that families didn't miraculously come back to life after a flaming carriage crash, and lost riches never magically reappeared.

Even though she knew it was an impossible dream, yearning stung the back of her throat. She felt for the shiny crystal button she wore on a string about her neck—the one remnant of her former life. It wasn't valuable, else she'd have bartered it away long ago. No, the button was simply a useless little trinket that she couldn't bring herself to part with.

Someday, I'll find a place to belong again. The old longing rose in her, and she savagely thrust it back down, then spat the taste of misery out of her mouth. Her home was gone forever, and that was the hard truth.

The hope of escaping Earth was harder to abandon, though, living as she did beneath the stitched shadows of takeoffs and landings from the largest spaceport in the galaxy. Every night she counted her small store of coins, but it was not enough. Never enough, not even for a berth to the moon.

"The moon," her young acquaintance Tipper had said,

rolling his eyes. "There's nothing up there but dust and the nob's castoffs. I want to go someplace real, like Patcheny or Blue Crumpet."

"Blue Crumpet's already full up," Diana had said. "I think Dahlia 7 is the planet for me."

They'd had the conversation at least a dozen times. Tipper's voice always held a longing that Diana had learned to hide—but then, for all his cockiness, he was still a child. Still dreaming the child's dream of space, the blackness full of stars and possibility. A million futures to choose from.

The reality, though, was this mucky alley, and the ominous silhouettes of two burly figures blocking the light.

Diana whirled, to find the other end of the alley guarded by a gaunt, black-clad man known as Pick and a smirking girl holding a knife. Breggy's crew, they were— members of the biggest gang in Southampton. And a pack of trouble, no question. Ever since the new leader had come into power, he'd been working to eliminate all the independents from the streets.

So far, she and Tipper and a few others had held out, refusing the bribery, nursing their bruises from the beatings. But Breggy wasn't giving up. The knowledge left a hollow hole in her gut.

"Hey, ho, Diver," the girl called. "Time for a bit of a chat."

Damnation. Diana knew better than to linger by the docks. She'd been a fool, and getting distracted by ships was no excuse.

"Don't know as we have anything to talk about," she

said, trying to keep her voice low and relaxed. "I paid Breggy my weekly tithe three days ago."

She glanced over her shoulder. The two thugs were sauntering down the alley toward her. There was no way out, except up, and she'd never been much of a climber. Her heart knocked loudly against her ribs.

"That's the thing." The girl ran a thumb along the length of her knife. "Terms just changed."

Diana bit back her words of protest. There was no arguing with the gangs, not in the stews of London, and not here. Either you paid or you ended up with a knife across your throat one dark night. Or the third option, which she'd never take: agree to join the unsavory crew.

She took a few steps toward the girl and Pick, away from the thugs at her back.

"How much?" Diana asked, her stomach clenching at the implications.

She was eking out a living and able—barely—to put a few coins by now and again. Someday, somehow, she'd escape the slums. But without a bit of the ready, it would be that much harder.

"Give us your purse, and we'll say." Pick held out his hand.

Reluctantly, she unfastened the pouch belted on under her shirt. The heavy tread of the men behind her sent her forward a few more steps, but not fast enough. Without warning, her arms were pinned to her sides from behind. With this crew, struggling would only earn her a cuff across the face, so she seethed silently and waited.

The other thug pulled the purse from her hand and

gave it to Pick. He opened it, a look of disdain on his face as he prodded through the contents.

"This is all you've got? A sorry showing, for someone reputed to be as light-fingered as yourself, Diver."

"'Twas a slow morning," she said. No need to mention the second, smaller pouch around her ankle, where every third shilling went. If she was lucky, they wouldn't discover it.

The girl pushed a greasy hank of hair out of her face and peered into the pouch.

"Pitiful," she said. "This will barely cover your new tithe."

Diana blew a breath out through her nostrils. It could be worse.

"We'll expect at least this much every third day," the man added.

It *was* worse.

"I can't—"

"Shut it," the man next to her said, jabbing an elbow into her ribs. "Don't need no excuses."

Diana caught her breath and swallowed the rest of her words.

"Best get quicker with your work," the girl said. "Then again, you could always join up. Breggy would find a use for you."

No doubt he would—something far more dangerous than working an unsuspecting crowd. Something like breaking into mansions and stealing diamond necklaces, which would either get her hung or transported to one of the prison worlds.

She wanted off Earth, but not like that. Prisoners didn't

live long. They labored under terrible conditions, terraforming planets and moons for real colonists to occupy once they were fit for human habitation. Criminals were expendable.

"I'll keep on my own," she said. "No insult to Breggy, of course."

Pick narrowed his eyes. "We'll get you yet, Diver. Too proud for your own good."

He tucked the purse into his sleeve. They were done. Relief coursed through Diana, until he nodded at the man beside her.

"Teach him not to complain," he said.

"I never—"

The breath was driven from her lungs as the man's fist connected with her stomach. She wheezed and doubled over. Blinking away the tears of pain blurring her eyes, she saw that Pick and the girl had gone, leaving her to be pummeled in the alley.

For a moment, Diana thought of calling for help—but what good would that do?

She still had her parasol, though, and the second man had let go of her arms, probably so that he could get a whack in.

Whirling, Diana, swung her bundle up between the man's legs. It connected with a satisfying thump

He made a strangled sound and staggered back a pace.

"Bastard!" The other man grabbed her arm.

Diana wrenched free and raced for the end of the alley. If she made it to the dock, she could lose herself in the crowd. Almost there. A few more steps and she'd be out of the shadows of the buildings and into free, clear air.

She risked a look behind her. Despite the anger on their faces, the two thugs were slow. She'd be able to outrun them.

Then she ran into something solid, and fell back, landing in a pile of muck. Oh, she was in for it now.

"What's this?" asked the very tall, very muscled policeman who'd stepped into the alley just as she was bolting out.

"Nothing, sir," she said, scrambling to her feet and wiping her filthy hands on her trousers.

"Friends of yours?" He nodded to the two men, who'd turned and were quickly making for the other end of the alley.

As she watched, they ducked out and were gone. Probably waiting for her—but she had multiple routes back to the bolt hole she called home, and knew she could make it there without being seen.

Coming back out tomorrow, however, might prove to be a problem.

More immediate in her list of troubles, though, was the policeman standing in front of her, hands on his hips. She gave him a quick once-over. Trim, not like the paunch-bellied constable who'd had the dock patrol last. Young, too. His shiny new holobadge read *Byrne*.

If she ran, chances were more than good he'd catch her. Best to play it innocent.

"I'd never seen them before," she said. "I think they meant to rob me."

No need to mention that she'd just had her purse full of purloined money and trinkets stolen in turn.

The policeman's dark eyebrows rose. "Have you anything of value?"

"A bit of coin."

"And what's your business at the docks?"

She let a bit of wistfulness creep into her voice. "I like to watch the ships land and take off. Best view of the spaceport."

It wasn't actually true. She'd found a perfect vantage point on top of an abandoned building where she could *almost* see over the huge, Yxleti-built wall surrounding the spaceport. And there was one other spot near her hidey hole: a vacant lot where she could map the arcs and parabolas the gleaming ships scribed through the blue.

Byrne's expression softened the tiniest bit.

"It's not safe down here," he said. "Especially for a girl."

Diana forced herself not to take a step back. "Good thing I'm a boy, then."

"I didn't see it right away, but now I do." He reached for her arm, and she twisted away from his grasp.

"Don't touch me." Stars, but she was in danger.

Only Tipper knew her secret—he'd caught her wrapping her chest one morning, and she'd sworn him to secrecy. Hopefully, the lad wouldn't betray her. It was beyond worrisome that some fresh-minted copper could see her as she was.

Blowing out a breath, he let his hand drop to his side. "There are places you can go, you know. The laundries—"

"Aye, where the girls drop like flies from overwork." Her throat tightened at the thought. "I'm not doing anything wrong."

The roar of another spacecraft ascending filled the air.

They both glanced up. A sleek Frigate XV, taking tourists up to Venus, she'd bet coin on it.

As soon as the noise cleared, Byrne fixed his gaze on her again. "It's not right, though. Are you living on the street?"

"No," she lied. It was none of his business—and clearly he was too soft to be patrolling the Southampton docks. Time to turn that to her advantage and make her escape. "My mum's expecting me. She worries if I'm late. May I go?"

He narrowed his bright blue eyes. "You've a pretty way with words."

Diana shrugged. "Family's fallen on hard times."

It was true enough, seeing as how she was the last member of her immediate family, and it was a convenient explanation for her occasional slips into gentrified speech. When pressed, she'd say that her mother had been a governess to the nobs, and she'd grown up in a big house, learning their ways.

There was no point in admitting she'd been the daughter of a lord and lady. She'd tried that road already, and it led nowhere. Not when the family in question was all dead, and had turned out, lost their entire fortune. Her only uncle was long gone to the moons of Saturn, oblivious to the fact that his niece had survived the dreadful carriage crash.

No use crying over curdled cream, though. Best to throw it out and start fresh.

The smell of sewage drifted down the alley, and the policeman grimaced. Diana tried not to smile. He'd get used to the stenches of the docks soon enough.

"Very well," he said. "On your way. And stay out of trouble, miss."

"Don't ever call me that," she said, her voice low.

Before he could respond, she ducked past him and let the crowd swallow her up. She'd trouble enough on her heels without adding a meddling policeman into the mix.

CHAPTER 2

DEREK BYRNE WATCHED THE GIRL SLIP AWAY INTO THE patchwork throng at the docks. She'd lied to him several times over, he'd no doubt of that. But what could he do?

He slowly clenched his hands into fists, then released them.

Damnú, a part of why he'd joined the constabulary was to make a difference, to help people. Instead, he had to stand helplessly by, watching young women throw their lives away and young men like his brother Seamus—*no, don't think on that*—make bad choices with even worse consequences.

As the newest member of the Southampton police force, Derek was well aware he'd been given the worst patrol. When he started three weeks ago, he'd been confident in his ability to do his job, and do it well, but now he wasn't so sure. The last few days had been spent in apprehending pickpockets and, yesterday, dealing with a dead body washed up in the river. His partner, Cribbs, was older, and hardened from his years on the force. Cribbs didn't have much sympathy for Derek and his faith in the general goodness of humanity.

That faith was rather ironic, Derek had to admit. After everything that had happened, he shouldn't be worried over such things as a streetrat's safety. And yet, he couldn't seem to stop himself from taking on the role of protector. It was part of his blood and bones to champion the underdog—be it a grubby girl, or his own people, despised and ground to ashes beneath the boot heel of the Empire.

One day, Ireland would be free of the British yoke—and he was there to help hasten that day along.

A commotion near one of the sidings pulled him from his musings, and he set off at a trot, hoping the young woman he'd been talking with wasn't involved.

As it turned out, she wasn't. A dispute over loading one of the ships moored at the pier had turned nasty, and one of the combatants took a knife wound to the arm before Derek and Cribbs could intervene. The fellow was taken off to the hospital, and Derek jotted a few notes on his handheld. He'd have to wait to see if the injured man wanted to press charges, but somehow he doubted it. Justice at the docks was rough and dirty, and seemed to operate under its own rules, with little heed paid to the Queen's laws.

Indeed, the whole of the West Quay area was ugly—worse than the run-down Dublin neighborhood he'd grown up in. Although, in his personal opinion, the Irish were harder in many ways than the English. Centuries of oppression would do that to a people.

"A nasty bunch, down here. Even worse than you

Paddys." Cribbs spit onto the grimy cobblestones. "Next year I get my promotion up to Lordswood. Can't hardly wait."

Derek held his tongue at the casual insult—he'd grown up hearing such things from the English all his life—and simply nodded at Cribbs's news. Everyone on the force knew that the rich neighborhood was the easiest patrol. No stabbings or muggings, and the vices were genteelly kept behind closed doors. Certainly there were thefts, but usually the culprits were found—often right among the servants working in the big houses.

"Look there." Cribbs nodded to a tall, thin man with bright red hair strolling through the crowd. He had an entourage with him—a disreputable-looking young woman, and two men dressed in black, with knives at their belts and the scars to prove they weren't afraid to use them.

"Who is it?" Derek asked.

"Breggy. Came recently to power. He controls the biggest gang in the whole port area, but keeps his own hands clean. Rumors are he's got connections in the gentry. Don't run afoul of him."

"I'll try not to."

As if aware they were watching, Breggy looked up. He smiled, sunlight glinting off a gold-capped front tooth, and tipped his hat. Cribbs scowled, and Derek narrowed his eyes.

Gangrunners were the lowest of the low, in his opinion. Unscrupulous, happy to use anyone as a tool to their own ends. He pitied anyone caught up in that kind of web. *Like Seamus. Like me.*

His secrets burned inside him, and he shoved them back down. For all anyone knew, he was simply the newest member of the Southampton police force. Not a man with an ulterior motive and ties to a certain radical organization.

"Do the Sisters of Mercy never come down here?" he asked Cribbs, thinking once again of the girl.

"They try. Breggy and his kind laugh at them, and they only save one or two off the streets a quarter. Maybe less. Who wants to go scrub cathedrals for the nuns when you can sleep free under the open sky? Least that's what the streetrats say."

"Not so pleasant in winter." Derek glanced at the sky, currently a deceptively placid blue.

Even now, near midsummer, the air was never truly warm. Squalls blew in regularly off the Solent, drizzling moisture over the docks and spaceport.

"Not at all," Cribbs agreed. "You'll want a good overcoat and boots, come October. We have to endure the same weather as the rats. Can't stay in The Frog and Whistle all day, after all."

Derek glanced at the pub fronting West Quay Road. It was the best of the several establishments scattered down the street; cleaner and with fewer chances of being murdered in a dark corner.

"Speaking of which," Cribbs continued, "it's lunchtime. Keep watch, and call for me if there's any more trouble in the next hour. We'll swap out, after."

Derek glanced down at his badge. With two taps, he could contact Cribbs. Three, and the badge would serve as a location device within a decent radius—certainly big enough to cover West Quay.

He nodded and didn't say anything about the amount of beer Cribbs was probably fixing to consume for lunch. Everyone did what they had to in order to get by.

CHAPTER 3

FOR THE NEXT FEW DAYS, DIANA TOOK EXTRA CARE SLIPPING in and out of her bolt hole—a sheltered corner in a derelict building near the spaceport wall. When the port had been built last century, the buildings directly around it had been demolished. The rest had been left to fall into ruin. Her current abode had likely been a lodging house, until the noise of the ships blasting off drove away the tenants.

Dawn warmed the sky as she folded her tattered woolen blanket away. A whiff of her own stink made her wrinkle her nose in disgust. Her routine of washing up in river water hauled home in a dented pail she'd found was inadequate over the long term. Luckily, there was a solution, though it had taken her months to discover it.

With a sigh, she pulled on her girl's clothing, fastened her hair up with twine and bits of blackened metal, and counted a few coins from her hidden store into the water-stained reticule she'd salvaged from the river's edge. Time to be a lady, or at least as much of one as she could manage.

Keeping to the early morning shadows, Diana made her

way out of the cluster of dilapidated buildings and into the bustle of the West Quay streets. In the morning, the port seemed fresher, the odor of garbage and rotting fish just a promise in the air, not a miasma brought to full bloom by the day's heat.

Midway along the quay, she was joined by a young boy with matted brown hair and a quick stride.

"Morning, Tipper," she said, giving him a sidelong smile and a twirl of her parasol.

"Aren't you the fancy one today, Di," he said, returning her smile with a chipped-tooth grin. "Where to?"

"The baths. Come along with me?"

He gave a shudder. "Never. It's unnatural, is what. Rain and the river are good enough for me."

"Suit yourself—but one day you'll change your tune."

"I doubt that." He clicked his tongue against his teeth. "Hey, seen the new copper on patrol? Word is he stopped two of Breggy's crew from robbing a fellow last night."

"Oh, that's not good." Breggy didn't like interference, and especially not from the law. "Do you think the new man won't be bribed?"

He'd struck her as an upstanding sort, with his broad shoulders and intent blue gaze. Of course, she knew better than to judge by appearances, but there was something about the new policeman—Byrne, that was his name—that made her think he wouldn't be easily cowed by Breggy and his ilk.

"Speaking of Breggy..." Tipper scuffed at the dirty cobbles with one worn boot. "I hear he's raising the tithe."

"Already did." Diana fought the urge to spit into the

street. In her current guise as a lady, it wouldn't be quite the thing. "Upped mine to twice a week."

Tipper glanced up at her, his eyes shadowed. "I can't pay that."

"I'll help you." It was foolish of her—but she couldn't imagine life in West Quay without at least one other stree-trat free of the gangrunners.

"I can manage," he said, shoving his hands in his pockets.

"Well, when you can't, tell me. I've a bit set by."

"That's for your berth to Dahlia 7, though. You can't use that!"

Leaving Earth was an impossible dream, for both of them, but she didn't have the heart to tell him so. At least one of them deserved the luxury of that hope—at least for a little while longer.

"I've got plenty of coin," she lied.

"Soon as we find the hidden passage into the port, we can stow away on a ship anyways." His grin was back in place. "Then Breggy and the gangs won't matter at all."

"Aye."

Another dream Diana was disinclined to tarnish. On the streets, dreams were sometimes the only things that kept a body going. Tipper would grow out of believing that particular fairy tale soon enough, and in the meantime she didn't mind helping him search the ruins for the mythical secret entrance to the spaceport.

She'd found her blanket that way, after all, and a comb only missing a few teeth.

The crowd thickened as they neared the bridge over the River Itchen. The smell of onions clashed with some nob's fancy perfume, and she wrinkled her nose. Though she had to admit she was doing her part to add to the general stench of humanity.

She glanced at Tipper. "Sure you're not coming?"

He halted and shook his head. "Never. Good pickings, Di."

"You too, Tip." She dipped him a little curtsy, then turned and blended with the pedestrians traveling over the Half Shilling bridge to Itchen.

A few months after hopping the rails to Southampton, she'd overheard two women talking in horrified tones about the Turkish baths across the river. Diana didn't care overmuch about the reputation of the baths—or her own, had she one to protect. But she did care about washing off the weeks of grime crusting her skin.

Of course, she had to go in girls' clothing, but on her first trip to the baths, she'd discovered there was no basis to the shocking gossip. Instead of a steamy hive of depravity and heathen sin, she'd found a quiet, respectable bathhouse where, as long as she had the money, no one asked her any questions.

The only problem was the wall in the women's side where the blue mosaic tile was mislaid. The sight of the uneven rows and gaps made her twitchy, so she always kept her back to it when she was in the warmth of the water. Other than that, it was a blessedly quiet haven.

It didn't hurt that there was a bustling marketplace near the baths, where Diana could recoup the bathhouse entry fee. She'd made a habit of bathing, then going to purchase a cup of strong Turkish coffee and roaming the bazaar, alternately taking in the colorful sights and rich smells, and nicking a bit of coin from stray pockets and purses. Never enough to raise the ire of the gangrunner on that side of the river, of course.

Because of the various risks, though, she only allowed herself the luxury of the Turkish baths once every few months. This time, when she emerged clean and calm from the women's side of the baths, she discovered she wasn't the only West Quay denizen to take a jaunt to the other side of the river.

Standing near the main entrance was the policeman, Officer Byrne. He was speaking earnestly with the turbaned man who owned the baths, while taking notes on his handheld.

Diana halted, but it was too late. Byrne's gaze rose to fix on her, and there was no mistaking the flash of recognition in his eyes.

Curse it! Now it would be impossible for her to deny she was a girl. No man would ever emerge from that side of the baths. They were very strictly maintained and chaperoned.

She pulled back into the shadows of the tiled portico, but there was only one way out. True, she could retreat back into the baths, claiming she'd left something behind, but she suspected that Byrne would only wait her out.

Besides, Breggy would demand his next portion later that day. She had little time to waste in trying to hide from overly perceptive policemen. No, it would be best if she simply marched right past Officer Byrne. If he tried to follow, she could lose him in the bazaar.

Suiting action to thought, she straightened her shoulders and crossed the patio, keeping her open parasol held at a precise fifty-degree angle between them. Just as she thought she'd pass him by unscathed, the policeman held out his hand.

"One moment, miss," he said.

She could run for it, certainly, but something stopped her. She was reluctant to cause a disturbance at the baths that have proven to be such a haven for her, and, in truth, she sensed Byrne meant her no harm. Perhaps if she calmly complied with his request, he would leave her be.

Halting, she tipped her battered parasol back so she could see his face.

When he met her eyes, an odd expression crossed his features. She blinked, and it was gone. No doubt he was recalling seeing her in boy's clothing and trying to reconcile the idea of her in trousers.

"Yes?" she asked, bringing a bit more of her highborn haughtiness to bear than she usually showed on the streets.

"I beg your pardon, but I'd like a word with you."

"Is there a problem?" the proprietor asked. "Other than what we were discussing earlier?"

"No." Byrne tucked his handheld away. "No problem."

"Very good. I will let you go about your business then." The man gave him a bow.

To her surprise, Byrne returned the salutation. It wasn't like the coppers to pay much heed to the customs of foreigners on their shores.

Then again, the new policeman had a clear Irish accent —and to many British, the Irish were as bad as the Turks, or worse.

Byrne turned to her as soon as the proprietor had gone.

"Miss," he began, then paused, his eyes narrowing slightly. "I believe I don't know your name."

Diana hesitated. Certainly she wasn't going to introduce herself as Miss Diana Smythe—but neither did the moment seem to warrant her street name of Diver.

"I'm Diana," she finally said. After all, there was no use in her continuing to pretend she was a boy. "You can call me Di," she added, with a pointed look.

The last thing she needed was a new-minted policeman calling out her true name in West Quay, and putting her in even greater danger.

"I'm Derek Byrne," he said. "You can call me—"

"Officer Byrne," she said. "Pleased to meet you, but I really must be on my way."

She strode through the opening in the wall enclosing the baths, exchanging a brief nod with the guard on duty there. Unfortunately, Byrne came after her—not that she really thought she'd be able to escape him that easily.

"I've a few questions for you," he said.

"Oh?" She shot him a look. "Is this to be an interrogation? I assure you, I'm guilty of nothing except desiring a bath."

He had the grace to flush a little. "It's about West Quay. And the gangs."

"Oh." Her steps faltered. "I've nothing to say about that."

It was dangerous. Too dangerous, to discuss street business with a policeman. If Breggy or the other gangrunners found out, she'd be dead in the river by morning.

"Please," he said. "I'd treat you to lunch."

Her stomach clenched at the thought. The last true meal she'd had was four days ago—a hot beef sandwich she'd bought fair and square. Before Breggy upped the tithe. Since then, she'd been living off apples stolen off the back of the vendor's cart, and the stale ends of bread the baker threw out. When she could beat the other streetrats to them.

"Very well," she finally said. "But we can't meet anywhere near the port."

At least she was in disguise as a young lady, and in a different quarter than the wharf rats usually frequented.

"Of course not." He sounded insulted. "We can go to one of the coffeehouses nearby."

"As long as it serves women." Not all of them did, she knew. Usually she bought her cup from a cart vendor. Cheaper that way, too.

"Trust me to know my business, Diana."

"Di," she corrected. "If you can't get that right, I'm not telling you a thing."

Not that she would reveal much, anyway. She'd just eat his food and say vague things about West Quay. Certainly she could ramble on for as long as it took to fill her belly. No streetrat owed a policeman anything. Ever.

CHAPTER 4

DEREK HAD BEEN KEEPING AN EYE OUT FOR THE LAST several days, wondering if he'd ever see the girl again or if the street had swallowed her up and would spit her mangled body back out in an alley or under a pier.

But he never expected to spot her coming out of the women's side of the Turkish baths in Itchen. So much for her claims of being a boy. He'd caught her out now, and no excuses.

To her credit, Diana—Di, he must remember—accepted her unmasking with good grace, and what's more, to his surprise, she agreed to have lunch with him.

There was a pinched look of hunger about her mouth he wanted to ease, though he suspected he was in for more lies and half-truths in return. Still, he felt surprisingly gallant as he escorted her across the street to the small coffeehouse mostly frequented by the Ottoman populace of Southampton.

There were enough English, however, both men and women, for their presence to go unremarked. He hoped.

Though Di hadn't spelled it out, he knew well enough it was trouble for a streetrat to be seen meeting with a policeman.

He glanced at her as she settled herself with ladylike grace at the small table. *Damnú*, she didn't look like a common beggar—especially now that she'd scrubbed the grime off. Her dark blonde hair escaped in wisps from beneath her bonnet, and her gray eyes regarded him from a fine-boned face tanned browner from the sun than was proper.

How could anyone mistake her for a boy? Certainly she was slender, but her figure curved in interesting places—

"Ahem." She gave him a pointed look. "I'd thank you to stop staring at my bosom, Officer Byrne."

He quickly averted his gaze and cleared his throat. "My apologies, miss. Er, Di."

Thankfully, the serving man arrived, and the next few moments of ordering strong Turkish coffee and lunch allowed Derek to regain his equilibrium.

When the server left, Derek leaned forward, determined to be a model of professionalism.

"How long have you lived in West Quay?" he asked.

Di folded her arms. He noticed two holes in her gloves, and several other places where the cloth had been darned.

"Long enough," she said.

"And you live with your mother?"

"Yes. She's ill, so I do what I can to support us."

She was an accomplished liar, but Derek had always been able to sense when someone wasn't telling him the truth. His granny said it was a Gift, but his Pa had just called it shrewdness. Either way, it served him well.

Unless people didn't believe *him*. His stomach knotted with memory, the echo of his brother's death, and it took him a moment to focus on the fact that Di was still speaking.

"She was a governess up in London, before her employer… Well. I'm sure you know the story. When they discovered she was pregnant, she lost her position. But she gained me." Diana gave him a shaky smile.

She sounded very convincing, but the tale was a touch too pat. Still, he nodded as if he believed her.

"She's lucky to have you," he said. "I take it you've been able to steer clear of the gangs then?"

"Yes." Her answer was a shade too quick.

"I hear the main runner's name is—" Derek broke off as their meal and coffee arrived. The smell of the beverage filled the air, rich and strong, and he inhaled appreciatively.

"I'd have thought you a tea drinker," Di said.

"What, because I'm Irish? You're English—I could say the same of you."

She shrugged. "I like either one, when I can get it."

Which wasn't often, he'd wager. Any hot beverage would be a luxury for a streetrat.

"Go ahead, eat. I see how you're looking at those kebabs."

Di peeled off her gloves, and he noted her fingers trembled slightly as she reached for the food. Despite her restraint, there was a desperate quality to her chewing that told him she was far hungrier than he'd guessed.

Thoughtfully, he took a sip of his deliciously strong coffee and decided he didn't need any lunch, after all.

It seemed rude to make her answer his questions while she was trying to eat, so he cast about for a topic of conversation. Of course, the main thing to talk about in Southampton was the spaceport, the busy heart of the British Galactic Empire. Which was ultimately why he was there.

In fact, just yesterday he'd received a coded message inquiring about his progress in that regard. Unfortunately, even as a constable, it was hard to gain access to the inner workings of the spaceport. So much of his time was spent with the problems of West Quay.

"Quieter on this side of the river," he said, "without the ships blasting off right over our heads. I didn't expect the sky to be so busy, when I took this position."

She swallowed a bite. "I like it."

"I do, too." To his surprise, he found it was true. "There's something thrilling about seeing all the ships coming in and out."

"Wish the spaceport wasn't so walled in," Diana said, setting her kebab and bread down to take a gulp of coffee.

Derek cocked one eyebrow. "So you could stow away to some exotic planet?"

Her hunger-hollowed face flushed, and he knew his words had met their mark. Without the impenetrable Yxleti-made wall and impossibly tight security, the spaceport would certainly be overrun by stowaways and smugglers, not to mention refugees begging berths off-planet.

There was enough of that already in West Quay outside the two gates of the port.

"Ever thought of trying to work passage out or enlisting as a colonist?" he asked.

She scoffed under her breath. "I know what happens to indentured laborers, and I've no skills to offer as a colonist."

Neither of them mentioned the other way to leave Earth: transported as a convict to a penal colony and assigned to hard labor for life.

"Besides," she added hastily, "I can't leave my mum, and she's too ill to travel."

Ah, she'd almost forgotten her story. He hid his smile. Despite her wariness, Diana was dropping her guard around him. Whether it was his Irish charm, or his innate ability to set people at ease, he was glad of it. This young woman intrigued him—more than she should. Then again, he'd long ago learned to trust his instincts.

The server came around with more coffee, the aroma blending with the smell of spices wafting from the kitchen. Just as he began to pour, a woman called to him in fluid Arabic from the doorway. Distracted, he turned slightly away. The stream of hot liquid shifted and Derek flinched as it landed on his forearm.

Except... it didn't. Somehow, Diana had lifted her cup and intercepted the pour. Instead of splashing all over his arm, the coffee landed neatly in her cup.

"So sorry!" The serving man lifted the enameled coffee server, then stared a moment at Diana, who was taking a calm sip from her now-full cup.

Not a drop of coffee showed on the tablecloth, or on Derek's sleeve.

"No harm done," Derek said, blinking with the aftermath of his surge of adrenaline.

As soon as the server left, he leaned forward across the table.

"How did you do that?" he asked Diana in a low voice.

She shrugged. "I could see it was going to be a mess. Easier just to intercept the stream."

"Yes, but how?"

"In my cup." She tilted her head at him, her tone suggesting he was being rather obtuse.

He sighed and sat back in his chair, taking a moment to breathe deeply. Perhaps what Diana had just done was not so extraordinary after all. Catching the coffee so deftly could be attributable to luck or timing.

Still, she had extraordinary reflexes, even for a streetrat.

Conversations in both English and Turkish eddied around them, and he noted that her plate held only crumbs.

"I'm not much in the mood for lunch," he said, sliding his falafel toward her. "Please, take it."

She glanced at him, and he was struck by the clarity in her eyes.

"I couldn't," she said, lacing her fingers tightly together as though to keep herself from reaching for the food.

"'Twould be a pity to leave it to be thrown out," he said. "I have more a taste for baklava, anyhow."

"Sweet tooth?"

"Aye."

The memory came, unbidden, of filching Ma's butter cookies fresh from the oven, burning his mouth on them from eating them before they were cool. She'd yell at him and Seamus to get out of the kitchen and threaten to whack them with her spoon.

"If you're sure, then." Diana's gaze went to his food.

"I am."

While she was eating, he flagged down the server and ordered a large plate of baklava. A few pieces would do well enough to tide him over until supper, and he'd no doubt Diana could do with a sweet. He'd press any leftovers on her to take home to her "mother."

"I want to ask you something." He flicked on his handheld and set it on the table between them. The screen showed a drawing of a strange symbol: three lines scored across a precise triangle. "Have you seen this image before?"

She leaned over and peered at it, not a flicker of recognition on her face. "I haven't. What is it?"

"Copy of a tattoo—the only identifying mark on a body we fished out of the river last week."

She lifted one shoulder in a shrug. "Bodies are tossed in the Itchen all the time. Why's this one different?"

"It just is."

He took his handheld and slipped it back into his pocket, reluctant to divulge police details. Like the fact the body had been wearing expensive clothing and two gemmed rings, which meant it wasn't an ordinary steal-and-stab. Plus, there were no overt signs of violence on the corpse. Derek was betting on poison, and maybe it was just a dispute among the nobility, but his intuition said otherwise.

Cripps wanted to close the case and be done with it, but there had been another clue besides the tattoo. One of the man's rings had a few words etched around the inside of the band. In Arabic, which was why Derek had come to the

Ottoman district. The proprietor of the baths was discreet and, though almost no one knew it, in the employ of Her Majesty's Secret Service. He'd apparently passed a vital bit of information to the force several years ago, when the safety of the Empire was at stake.

Derek had given the man the ring, under pretext of writing out a minor citation. The proprietor had warned him not to come back, however, insisting he'd be in contact as soon as he had any information.

So now it was down to waiting, which Derek did not enjoy. At least he could distract himself with Diana's surprisingly interesting company.

The baklava came, deliciously sticky with honey, and he attempted once again to find out more about the underbelly of West Quay.

"I hear a fellow named Breggy runs the dockside gangs," he said quietly. "Heard of him?"

Her expression a little too blank, Diana glanced at him. "Surely—enough to steer clear of the fellow."

Derek wiped his hands clean, then gave her a mild look. "And how is it, exactly, that you're making a living?"

"Not working for a gangrunner," she said, with enough heat that he believed her. "Anyhow, I need to be off to check on Ma."

She gave the half-empty plate of baklava a regretful glance.

"Take some to her," he said. "I'll have the server wrap it in waxed paper."

He wanted to insist he accompany her back across the river, too, but though she'd accept the leftover pastry, he knew she wouldn't take his company.

It was hard to remember that this poised young woman was actually a streetrat going by the name of Diver. Not when the curve of her cheek was so feminine. And her accent, when she was relaxed and well-fed, veered toward the posh.

"Right then." She stood. "Meet me outside. I'm going to change."

"Change?" he asked, but she whisked off, ignoring his question.

Derek paid for the meal, then took the packet of neatly wrapped baklava outside. He strolled down the block, unsure of what Diana had been planning. Had she decided not to take the leftovers after all, and was even now laughing at having given him the slip so easily?

"*Hist.* Byrne, over here." The whisper came from the dark shadows of a nearby alley.

Derek sidled over and glanced into the narrow recess between the buildings. A boy skulked there, grubby-faced and wearing trousers. The transformation was so complete that Derek blinked for a moment—even though he knew it was Diana beneath the ragged clothing, her hair hidden under the cap.

"Di?"

"'Course." Even her voice had changed back to the rougher syllables of the street. "Got my package?"

He handed it over. All the words he wanted to say were clogged in his throat, kept back by common sense. She didn't need his admonition to be careful and would no doubt find his concern insulting.

It was even surprising to him.

"See you across the river," he managed.

She tucked the sweets into the cloth-wrapped bundle she carried—probably her skirts, he realized—then flashed him a quick smile and darted away without a word of thanks. A moment later he was left staring at the empty, soot-colored wall, left with only the memory of her grey eyes and the unsettling surety that there was far more to her than he'd guessed.

CHAPTER 5

Diana doubled around and waited for Byrne to head back across Half Shilling bridge before following at a leisurely distance. Not that she thought he'd try to shadow her home, but caution was a lesson learned early on the streets, and one she wasn't about to abandon over a full belly and a packet of leftover pastry.

She floated along with the foot traffic, snagging a coin here, a kerchief there. Small things, and mostly just to keep herself amused as she went.

Once they gained West Quay and she was satisfied the policeman was going about his rounds, she headed off to Tipper's favorite corner. Sure enough, he was there, occupying a nook near the spaceport's service entrance. He wore a dingy bandage around his hand, making it appear to end in a stump, and a piteous look that always coaxed a few coins from the softer-hearted among the spaceport's laborers.

She strolled by without looking at him, then nipped

around the corner. Of course he'd seen her—not much escaped those sharp eyes. When he was ready, he'd empty his bowl of coins into his pockets and join her.

In the meantime, she leaned back against the dingy bricks and thought about her lunch with Byrne; their conversation, the food, the kindness he'd shown her. Each moment glowed, the whole like a handful of marbles catching the light. She hadn't felt like that in forever. So... *herself.*

Which was, of course, a dangerous thing to be. Bad if anyone discovered she was a noble-born girl, and worse if Breggy or his gang found out about her peculiar talents. The gangrunner was as clever as he was cruel, and quickly gaining a reputation for turning every tool to his hand. Or streetrat to his advantage, no matter the cost.

She'd given too much away, earlier, when she'd caught the spilled coffee, but she hadn't wanted to see Byrne scalded. Although she'd passed it off as nothing, she worried that he hadn't quite believed her.

Ah well, there was naught she could do about it now except keep her head down. Their paths wouldn't cross again, if she could help it. Streetrats and coppers had no business together, unless it was of the most unsavory sort —snitches or slags. She wouldn't stoop to that, and she didn't think Byrne would, either.

Tipper limped around the corner, then straightened and pulled off the bandage covering his hand.

"You look too clean," he said, wrinkling his nose.

"It won't last. I brought you something."

She wasn't entirely sure why she was sharing her

bounty with Tipper. They had a rough camaraderie, certainly, but it wasn't wise to get too close on the streets. *It's for my own protection,* she told herself. If Tipper felt he owed her, he'd be less likely to spill her secrets.

She held out the packet of baklava, watching as he took it and peeled back the waxed paper. He dipped his head and sniffed, a look of bliss crossing his face as the aroma of cinnamon and butter drifted up from the pastry.

"Smells like heaven." He took a bite, then nodded vigorously. "Tastes like it, too," he said through a full mouth.

He extended the packet to her, but she shook her head. "I had plenty. Eat up."

It didn't take much urging. Tipper practically inhaled the pastry. When it was gone, he licked the paper clean of crumbs, then his fingers.

"Pistachios, honey, a bit of cardamom. Like eating pure sunshine." He sighed and slid down the wall to sit, legs splayed in front of him. "If that's what's on the other side of the river, mayhap I'll come along next time. As long as you don't try to clean me up."

"I'd never."

He folded the waxed paper into a small square and tucked it in his pocket. Then his head lifted, eyes widening as he looked past her. Diana whirled, stiffening at the sight of Breggy himself sauntering down the street.

Tipper scrambled to his feet, and they both turned to run, but Breggy's black-clad boys were there between one heartbeat and the next. The one called Pick dug his fingers into Diana's arm, while another caught Tipper by the shoulder.

"Not going to run off from an audience with his majesty now, are ye?" Pick asked, his voice hard.

"Course not," Diana lied. Always best to play along with their little games.

"I'm most pleased to hear it." Breggy came to a halt before them. "How fortunate to find the two of you together. It makes collecting my tithe so much easier."

His smile glinted gold, and held not a trace of warmth. His eyes were colder still, pebbles of ice and silt.

"Give it over." The man holding Tipper gave him a shake.

Mouth twisting, Tipper reached into his trousers and brought out a small linen bag. "This's all I got."

Breggy took it and weighed it thoughtfully in his hand. "I'm afraid that's only a fraction of what you owe, young man. Surely you have more concealed about your person."

"I don't—" Tipper's words ended in a yelp as he was shoved roughly up against the wall. The bricks scraped his cheek, raising a welt on his skin.

"Search him," Breggy said. "Be rough."

The man holding Tipper laughed. It wasn't a pleasant sound. Nearby pedestrians averted their eyes and crossed the street. They knew better than to intervene in gang justice—especially when it grew violent.

"Stop." Diana shrugged free of Pick's grasp and stepped forward. "I'll pay for the both of us."

"Di—ouch—don't." Tipper's voice wavered, and she was reminded again of how young he was.

"Shut it," she said to him, digging through her pockets for her hidden purse.

Breggy's icy gaze shifted to her and she tried not to

shiver. "A deplorable weakness, Diver. Hasn't the street taught you to care only for yourself?"

"Here." She held up the purse, a ragged velvet thing with nearly all the nap rubbed off.

By all the stars, she hoped her store of coins would be enough to save them both from a beating. Her bruises from last time had barely healed.

Breggy turned his palm up and she dropped the purse in the hollow of his manicured hand.

"Hm," he said, still looking at her. "Haven't been holding back on us, have you?"

"I was across the river," she said.

Something flashed in his eyes. "Daring of you, to work another gang's turf. I approve of your initiative."

No doubt he approved of taking proceeds from his rivals, too. She waited, breath shallow, while he opened the purse and pushed the coins about inside. They made a dull clinking and for a moment she wished she'd taken more risks in her pickpocketing.

But increased profits also meant increased danger. No matter how friendly Officer Byrne had seemed, he'd pop her in the clinker without an eyeblink if she were caught.

"Almost enough," Breggy said.

Before Diana could ask what more they had to give, he turned and casually backhanded Tipper across the face. His diamond rings scored two lines of blood on the boy's cheekbone. White-faced, Tipper bit his lip, but she saw the wetness in his eyes.

"You..." Diana swallowed the hot insults pressing against her teeth. She trembled with the effort of holding them in, even as rage flashed through her like lightning.

Don't cross Breggy, or you'll be floating in the river, she reminded herself.

"Now we're paid up," the gangrunner said. "This time."

"Bow," Pick said, grabbing Diana's shoulders and forcing her into an awkward bend forward. "Thank his majesty for his mercy."

She mumbled something, blood still prickling with white-hot anger. *Thank* him? Oh, Breggy was getting worse every day.

Tipper bowed, too, and croaked out a stilted word of graditude.

"You may rise," Breggy said. "Don't fight too long, stree-trats. Easier if you accept the inevitable, and join me now. I'll treat you well, I promise."

His promises were as empty as the air, but misgivings pooled at Diana's feet like oily puddles. How much longer could she and Tipper stay clear of the gangrunner's clutches?

They watched silently as Breggy strode away, flanked by his men. Once he was out of sight, Diana turned to Tipper and blotted the blood from his face with her sleeve.

"Oh, Tip," she said, overcome by a rush of fear-tinged affection.

"Don't worry." Despite his brave words, he leaned against her. "I'll find that secret entrance to the spaceport, and then we'll be out of Breggy's reach. You'll see."

"I hope you find it soon," she said, trying to sound positive, though all her confidence, all her hope, was withering like tender flowers under a hard frost. Soon enough she'd have nothing left but a handful of slimy, blackened stems and colorless petals.

The roar of a ship taking off made the ground tremble slightly under their feet. Silently, she and Tipper lifted their faces and watched it rise over the spaceport, a silver and red dream escaping gravity. Flying far, far away from where they stood.

CHAPTER 6

Derek strode through the Southampton Spaceport market, keeping an eye out for trouble. And the slight figure of a dark-blond pickpocket. He found the former, of course—in the first fifteen minutes of his shift he'd already broke up a fistfight and rousted a drunk slumped half-asleep in a doorway—but there was no sign of the latter.

He supposed it was for the best. If he caught Diana at her trade, he'd have to take her in. Down here at the docks, a policeman couldn't get a reputation for being soft.

"Stop! Thief!" The call made him whirl, and he sucked in his breath as he saw someone dart through the crowd.

The culprit was too short and thin-faced to be Diana. Derek let the air out of his lungs in whoosh and sprinted after the boy. Just as the lad was about to dash down the mouth of a stinking alley, Derek caught him by the collar.

He grabbed the boy's arm for good measure and turned him about.

"Let me go," the boy said, then stilled as he took in

Derek's uniform. A flash of fear crossed his face, quickly replaced by a piteous expression.

"Turn out your pockets," Derek said.

"Please, sir—I've done nothing wrong." The boy was a good actor, summoning the touch of a quaver to his voice. But Derek wasn't fooled.

"Now," he said, not loosening his grip.

The lad heaved a sigh and pulled his trouser pockets inside-out. As Derek suspected, there was nothing inside.

"Y'see, sir? Now may I go?" the boy asked.

"Off with the coat," Derek said.

The boy slid one arm out of his frayed sleeve. Before he could peel out of the garment and bolt, Derek transferred his grip to the boy's shoulder His captive gulped, then slowly finished removing the coat.

Two coins pinged onto the cobblestones, along with a half-eaten currant bun. Derek snagged the coat and gave it a shake. Another coin fell out, and an apple that rolled away into the mucky gutter beside the street.

"Where'd they come from?" Derek asked mildly.

He was sorry to see, up close, that the boy was quite young; a lad of about ten, if he had to guess. Two scabbed-over cuts welted the boy's cheek, with a dark bruise beneath. Another set of bruises showed on his wrist, where someone had grabbed him roughly.

"I found 'em," the boy said, his gaze on the bruised apple lying in a pool of slime.

Another good thing tossed into the street to become trash. Derek pushed down the pity rising in him. He knew when he signed up for the force the job it wouldn't be easy.

"I have to take you in," Derek said. "Stealing's a criminal offense."

The boy bit his lip and looked on the verge of tears—genuine this time.

"If there's no proof, you can't keep me," he said.

Still holding him by the shoulder, Derek bent and scooped up the coins. "We can hold you for a full day. If no charges are brought during that time, then we'll have to release you. What's your name?"

"Tipper." The boy swallowed. "Could I have my bun?"

At Derek's nod, he snatched up the bread, then brushed it off against his trousers and took a bite. Despite the fact that it was evidence, Derek let the boy gobble it down. Then, still holding firmly to his captive, Derek towed him back into the marketplace.

The coins the boy had pilfered probably couldn't be traced at this point, but the apple could only have come from one place.

Mrs. Jones stood in front of her fruit and vegetable cart, arms crossed, eyes narrowed as Derek hauled his captive up.

"Have you seen this boy before?" Derek asked. At his side, Tipper hung his head low.

"Aye." Mrs. Jones's voice was hard. "He's nicked from me more than once, the thief. Couldn't catch him 'til now."

Derek didn't bother mentioning that he was the one who'd caught the boy, not Mrs. Jones.

"Do you want to press charges?" he asked her.

"And how! Lock him up for good. One less streetrat nibbling away at my profits."

Tipper shivered. No doubt the boy was aware his fate

would be years of indentured servitude, followed by transportation once he came of age. Derek pushed away another unwelcome twinge of sympathy.

"Come down to the station to fill out the forms," he said to Mrs. Jones. "We'll set a trial date."

The boy was clearly guilty, and there would be no one to speak on his behalf, but the motions of justice would be carried out. Even if the conclusion was foregone.

"I'll just do that," Mrs. Jones said, jamming her rumpled hat more securely atop her head. "Soon as I close up for the day."

"I'll look for you later," Derek said. "Good day, ma'am."

He towed the boy through the marketplace. Though no one stared outright, he could sense the vendors' satisfaction at seeing a thief in custody, the rustle of concern as other street urchins caught wind of the arrest.

He wondered if word would get back to Diana, and if she knew the boy.

Southampton Port Station was small and dingy, with two holding cells. One already held a drunk and disorderly, sleeping off his bender. Derek put the boy in the other cell, which didn't smell quite so strongly of vomit.

Tipper looked small and scared as he sat on the thin cot, hugging his legs. There were no words of comfort Derek could give. He couldn't guess at the many possibilities that had put the boy out on the streets at a young age—but the law was the law. And woe to anyone who fell afoul of it.

Swallowing back bitter memories, Derek turned away from the dank cell, trying to ignore the tear he'd seen shining on Tipper's cheek.

~

"HE WHAT?" DIANA STARED AT THE GRUBBY GIRL WHO'D brought her the information that Tipper had been caught stealing that very afternoon.

"Taken." The girl's voice was so soft, Diana had to lean close to hear it.

"Are you sure it was Tipper?" she asked. Her lungs clenched tight. *Not Tipper, please.*

The girl nodded, her expression wary behind her matted tangle of hair. "Saw 'im grabbed wif me own eyes."

"Thank you for bringing me the news." Terrible as it was.

Even as her heart wailed with silent despair, Diana dug into her purse and pulled out a thin coin to give the girl. Information was valuable, and she had left her begging spot in order to bring Diana word. One coin probably wouldn't make up for the lost income, but it would help.

The girl snatched it from her hand then darted away— almost more feral creature than child.

As soon as she was out of sight, Diana let out a hollow breath and slumped against the sooty brick wall at her back.

Tipper, in jail.

Her throat closed with grief at what that meant. Her best—her *only*—friend on the street, gone.

No.

She slowly closed her hands into fists. There had to be some way to save him, and she would find it. She must.

CHAPTER 7

IT WAS LATE, THE SKY SALTED WITH STARS, WHEN MRS. JONES finally stepped into the station. Derek's shift had ended two hours earlier, but something had made him stay. He'd ignored Cribbs's look and muttered comment that the new constable was soft.

Maybe so. But when Derek's gut told him to do something, he did it. He'd learned that lesson the hard way.

Silently, he'd handed Tipper a packet of chips from the pub, then took his own supper and pint of ale to the desk in the corner. The secretary had left a tablet waiting, the forms for Mrs. Jones to sign at the ready.

As evening fell, Derek turned up the gaslights—no fancy lightstrips for the Southampton Port Station. That kind of tech was reserved for the best parts of town, where such things wouldn't be stolen and resold on the gray market the moment a man's back was turned.

Finally, when he was considering giving it up and going back to his small flat, Mrs. Jones opened the featureless metal door and stumped over the threshold. She had a baleful glint in her eye as she glanced at the cell holding Tipper. He sat in dejected pose, head bowed over his folded arms.

"Good evening, Mrs. Jones." Derek rose. "Are you ready—"

"Nay." She spit the word out. "I'm dropping the charges." She clearly wasn't happy about it.

Tipper stiffened and carefully raised his head. Derek could see the wild light of hope kindling in his eyes. *Steady now*, he wanted to tell the boy. *Don't wish for too much, or the world will break your heart.*

"Are you, now?" he asked Mrs. Jones, keeping his voice mild. "Are you quite sure?"

"Not a bit of it." She made a sour face. "But I'm dropping them, all the same."

Tipper rose and went to the front of the cell, his small, pale fingers wrapping around the metal bars.

"Thank you," he said, his voice wavering.

"'Tisn't kindness, I'll have you know." Mrs. Jones made a fist and shook it at him. "If I see you anywhere near me cart again…"

"You won't never," he said. "I swear it."

Derek crossed his arms, thoughts circling rapidly through his head. What had made Mrs. Jones change her mind?

"Does this have anything to do with the gangs?" he asked. "Breggy?"

"Pah!" She spit on the floor.

It was none too clean to begin with, but Derek still sent a sidelong glance at the splotch of saliva.

"I'd never truck with scum like him," she said. "Are we done here?"

Derek nodded. He couldn't force Mrs. Jones to stay at the station, no matter the questions buzzing through him.

"Well, let 'im out." She scowled at the cell.

Derek set his palm to the lock. It hummed, scanning his prints, then the cell door clicked open. Tipper stood there, poised for flight, yet seeming unsure where he was flying to. It could easily enough be from the pan into the fire.

"Watch yourself," Derek said.

Relief on Tipper's behalf pooled in his belly—but it didn't mean the boy wouldn't land in jail again within the fortnight. On the streets, any reprieve was only temporary.

"It's not a trick?" Tipper asked, sending a glance to the station door.

Derek wondered the same thing. Was the gold-toothed gang leader waiting just outside, ready to indenture the boy into an endless servitude?

"I'll escort you out," Derek said, setting his hand on his taserclub.

"Git on with you." Mrs. Jones jerked her head at Tipper. "Let's be done with this."

She marched for the door, Tipper a small shadow behind her. Derek followed, his senses on high alert.

The night was clammy, the noxious odors in the air more pronounced without the distraction of daylight. Sewage, rot, the salt-tinged muck of ebb tide. He paused in the shadows of the station's doorway and scanned the street. No gang members seemed to be waiting in the stinking night.

Mrs. Jones grabbed Tipper's thin shoulder and hauled

him forward into the fitful glow of the nearest gas street-lamp. Eyes narrowing, Derek didn't step out of his concealment.

A figure dressed to blend with the dark detached itself from the mouth of a nearby alleyway. Despite the trousers and concealing hat, Derek recognized the form immediately: Diana.

She cocked her head, and Mrs. Jones let go of Tipper's shoulder. The boy scampered toward Diana, a grin spreading across his face.

"It's done," Mrs. Jones said.

"Thank you." Diana held out a purse.

The other woman snatched it from her hand. "Don't think you can short me, streetrat. I can always finger your friend again—this time for permanent."

"It's all there," Diana said, her voice cold. "Every shilling."

With a snort of contempt, Mrs. Jones shoved the purse into a pocket deep in her skirts. She gave Tipper a venomous look, then turned on her heel and stalked away.

"Oh, Di." Tipper flung his arms about Diana's waist.

She patted his back. Despite her smile, her expression was strained. Derek wondered how much had been in that purse, and just how she'd gotten it.

He moved silently out of the doorway, and Diana's head jerked up. She tensed for flight, but stilled when she saw his face.

"Bribery is also a criminal offense," he said calmly.

Tipper jumped back at the sound of his voice. "C'mon, Di," he whispered sharply. "Run!"

She took his hand in a reassuring grip, but her gaze met Derek's.

"I did what I had to," she said.

The sincerity in her eyes made his stomach do an odd little flip. How could this girl living on the streets have such a depth of character? He hated what he was about to do—but he was a sworn officer of the law.

"So must I," he said. "Come into the station."

"No," Tipper said, the edge of panic in his voice.

"Let Tipper go without a fuss," Diana said, "and I'll come. Shh, Tip, it's all right. He can't keep me."

It was debatable, but, curse the girl, she'd read Derek's intent well enough. He wasn't going to lock her up.

"I'm coming, too," the boy said bravely, though his face was pale.

The two marched forward like prisoners going to transportation. They could have run, of course, and there was little Derek could have done about that. But the unlikely connection between himself and Diana held. It was not trust, not quite. More just a sense that, beyond the roles of constable and streetrat, they had recognized one another as human.

Humanity. A liability, perhaps, here in the Southampton slums, but in the wider world, he could not help but be glad of it.

Derek showed them to his desk, and resisted the urge to pull out a chair for Diana. Probably Tipper knew her true gender, but there was no need to underscore it.

"Join me in a quick snack?" he asked, pulling out a few of the ration bars he kept in a drawer, in case of skipped meals.

Tipper, of course, gladly grabbed one. Diana, after a quick glance at Derek's face, took another. Instead of ripping the wrapper off and devouring it, as her friend was, she slipped it into a hidden pocket, then folded her hands in front of her.

"Good of you to rescue Tipper," Derek said. "I don't imagine it was cheap."

A pained look crossed her face, and she swallowed. "It wasn't so bad."

And the moon was made of green cheese.

"Am I going to hear about a burglary, tomorrow morning?" he asked mildly.

"No." Again, that clear-eyed gaze. "The money came from a bit I'd put by."

Tipper gasped and turned toward her. "No, Di! That was for your passage out."

She gave him a shaky smile. "I still have plenty left."

Tipper blinked at her. Derek wasn't sure if the boy heard the lie in her voice, but he certainly did. Buying Tipper's freedom had taken everything Diana had.

"Are you going to arrest me for bribing Mrs. Jones?" she asked.

"No," Derek said. "I could, of course, but I'll settle for information instead."

She pressed her lips together, then gave a quick nod. "What is it?"

"Breggy."

At the gangrunner's name, Tipper lifted an unconscious hand to the bruises on his face. So, these two were in trouble with the gangs. Made sense. Free agents on the street were dangerous to a gangrunner's control.

"He's been leader since last summer," Diana said.

Easy enough to guess what had happened to the last one, but Derek asked anyway. "And the leader before him?"

She lifted a shoulder in a half shrug. "Found washed up on the riverbank. Too soft, I suppose. He never recruited the streetrats hard as Breggy does."

"Aye," Tipper said. "We were right enough before the change-over. Now he's raised the tithe, and—"

Diana jabbed the boy with her elbow. "None of the copper's business, Tip."

Of course it was Derek's business—everything that happened in the underbelly of Southampton was. He filed the information away to mull over later, but it was evidence enough that Diana and her young friend were in trouble, and steering straight for more.

"The Quakers have a school in London," he said. "Open to anyone, and it's free."

Diana frowned, a bitter twist to her lips. "London's worse than here."

"'Sides, we have no way to get there," Tipper said.

"I'd pay your way." Derek's wages weren't substantial, but he could afford two train tickets to the city.

A streak of light speared the sky, followed by the roar of takeoff as another ship blasted off from the spaceport, straining to escape gravity. All three of them watched it go, until its glow was swallowed up by the rest of the night.

"We're going off-planet," Tipper said, bravado in his voice—as though if he spoke the words strongly enough, they would come true.

Diana set a hand on his shoulder, but said nothing.

"It's not safe for you here." Derek met her gaze. "You'd best be gone soon, the both of you."

The thought caused an odd little pang in his heart, but he ignored it.

"Maybe so." Her voice was soft. She glanced up at the stars, just a brief look, as if the answers were up there, somewhere.

And maybe they were—but he didn't know if either of them would ever get that far.

He cleared his throat. "Where's Breggy's den, then?"

"You can't go there." Tipper sounded aghast.

Diana nudged him again. "He won't, Tip. It's just information. The price of our freedom, remember?"

The boy subsided, and Diana took a breath.

"He's in the Wool House," she said.

Of course. The old stone building was near enough to a fortress. It was located perfectly for a gangrunner's needs, in the heart of the slums next to the quay.

"Can we go now?" Tipper asked, rocking up onto his toes, then back.

Diana met Derek's eyes and inclined her head, asking the same. In truth, he had no reason to keep them any longer.

"If you hear of anything I should know, I'd like you to tell me," he said.

Tipper let out a snort. "You know what the gangs do to informers?"

"Might be too late, Tip," Diana said. "Word'll get out about tonight."

"Then we lay low for a bit." The boy grinned with the resiliency of the young.

Another ship took off, and under the sound of its engines, Derek leaned forward. He clasped Diana's hand and gave it a quick squeeze.

"Be careful." He wanted to say more, but didn't know the words. The two of them were from different worlds, and there was nothing he could do to help her, despite trying. "My offer of tickets to London stands."

She returned the pressure of his grasp, then slipped her hand free.

"I know," she said. "Goodnight."

Quiet as the murmur of the river, she and Tipper stepped over the threshold into the darker shadows of the streets, and were gone.

A HEAVY SORROW PRESSED DOWN ON DIANA'S HEART AS SHE and Tipper left the station. Despite the boy's optimism, she truly didn't know what they were going to do next. *Lie low* was well enough, but they had no resources. Starve to death in their burrows, more like.

As they slipped through the back streets, she sifted through the options, trying to find a solution. Sludgy puddles reflected the light seeping into the sky. Sunrise was coming, and they were heading for their respective bolt holes none too soon.

The plain fact was, they both needed coin to buy food— no more stealing off the carts for Tip, that was certain. But if either of them ventured out into the crowds, Breggy would find them. When he did, there'd be no more escape.

Maybe she should take Derek's offer of tickets to London.

No. She'd be remembered there. Not by the coppers, mayhap, but by the gangs. When she'd first escaped the orphanage, she'd flaunted her abilities: counting money—

and cards—with a glance, predicting the movements of particularly rich-looking mark in a crowd, darting away from pursuers with only inches to spare between her and a fast-moving hansom cab.

She'd been looking for acceptance and approval—but her skills made her a valuable commodity. One of the gangrunners was set on turning her into a thief, sending her into the city's most prestigious houses to steal whatever she could. Another wanted to dress her like a flash nob—oh, the irony—and make her work Piccadilly right under the coppers' noses.

Diana couldn't read the future, but she was smart enough to see that either of those paths ended with her imprisonment and transportation. The gangrunners wouldn't care—they'd make good coin off her, then toss her away. Bribes to the police wouldn't outweigh the severity of the crimes they wanted her to commit. So she'd gotten away, careful to cover her tracks, and ended up in Southampton.

She wrinkled her nose against the stench of something dead wafting from a dank alley. Probably a rat, but she wasn't going in there to investigate.

"Are we going to London?" Tipper asked, as if reading her thoughts.

"I'm not sure." Of anything.

Don't trust me, she wanted to tell him. *Look at the mess I've made of things.* Except that she'd managed to pull him out of a jail cell, and that was worth something.

When she'd gone to Mrs. Jones she hadn't been sure the woman could even be bribed, but she had to try. Diana had brushed her hair out with her broken comb, then braided it, and donned her skirt and shawl. She'd say that Tipper was her younger brother, and she'd promised their Ma she'd look out for him. Plus, there was a goodly bag of coin to sweeten Mrs. Jones's sympathy.

Diana had held back tuppence and a few farthings, but all the shillings went into the small canvas bag she'd scrounged up at the water's edge. It was stained and smelled of mold, but it would do.

As it was, the amount was scarcely enough. Mrs. Jones had refused until Diana spilled the coins out into the woman's hands.

"Please, missus," she'd said, crying. "He's me only brother."

The tears had been easy to muster. Diana couldn't bear the thought of Tipper being taken away. Life on the streets was hard, but his punishment would be worse. Not to mention her own life, without him.

Finally, she'd prevailed, but fear had tightened her throat up until the moment Derek had unlocked the cell and let Tip go.

Now, however, there were almost no options left that didn't end in death or jail. For both of them.

The smooth, Yxleti-built wall of the spaceport rose a few blocks ahead, so strange in comparison to the crumbling brick and decayed mortar of the buildings around them. The abandoned square ahead was where they'd part, each to their respective hiding places.

In the tangle of the overgrown hedges, she paused and handed him the ration bar Byrne had given her.

"Keep your strength up," she said, ignoring the rumbling in her own belly.

"Don't worry." Tipper took the bar, then patted her arm. "We'll be all right, Di. See you in a bit?"

"Yes," she said, trying to sound cheerful. "I've a bit of bread and cheese we can have for breakfast."

And that was all.

She supposed they could try to kill and eat the rats, or try and fish something misshapen and dubious out of the Itchen, but her stomach turned at the thought. Still, it would be better than starving to death.

Breggy wouldn't let us starve. The thought came unbidden.

True—but he'd demand things she wasn't willing to give. Even if her life depended on it. It wasn't worth trading her little bit of freedom, no matter how hungry and desperate, for a certain and unsavory misery.

Tip gave her a jaunty wave, backlit by the rising sun, and strode off. A night in jail hadn't dampened his spirits overmuch, and she didn't know whether to smile or cry at that fact. The boy was so sure everything would come out right. But this wasn't a fairy tale.

Tasting the bitter salt of her swallowed tears, Diana waited in the hedge until she was satisfied they hadn't been followed. Then, carefully, she made her way to the ruins she called home.

The roar and shake of spacecraft blasting off had long since ceased to wake Diana from her ragged slumber. Her dilapidated corner in a falling-down building was scant shelter from the elements, but she'd learned to catch what rest she could.

A stealthy approach or a whisper of malice, however, would bring her awake in an instant, hand tight around the hilt of her makeshift dagger. It was just a jagged piece of metal she'd salvaged, with a knotted rag for a handle, but it was still a weapon.

Her father had had a gun, once, a light-pistol that could slice a man's arm off, or put a smoking hole in his chest at fifty paces.

Long gone, along with the rest of the remnants of her former life. Diana didn't even have a gold locket with her parent's picture, or a pocket watch with a loving inscription, or any of the tokens common to novels about abandoned girls seeking their long lost homes and families.

She was awake, woken by Tipper's light step—but she pretended to be asleep. The day was full of unanswerable problems she didn't want to rise and face: the grimy reality of the West Quay slums, the ships blasting off out of reach. And all her coin gone. She'd never make it back, now that Breggy had upped the tithe.

"Di, get up. I know you're awake."

A toe in her ribs made her roll over and open her eyes. Tipper stood there, silhouetted against the brightness. Behind him, clouds feathered the sky, and sunlight glowed on the grungy buildings. By her reckoning, it was two in the afternoon, or thereabouts. Used to be she knew down to the minute, but without a proper timepiece, she couldn't be sure.

"Go away, Tip. Wake me up later."

"Can't." The boy squatted down next to her and poked

her shoulder with a grimy finger. His grin shone bright as the sunlight. "I finally found it, Di!"

That woke her fully. She sat, letting her hole-filled woolen blanket drop from around her shoulders.

"What did—" She broke off as the roar of a blast-off filled the air.

Both she and Tipper looked up. From the sound of that lift, it was one of the bigger ships; maybe a Fauntleroy 220. The gleaming silver shape arced overhead, catching the light and shining, shining. It was a Fauntleroy, just as she'd guessed.

Soon after she'd arrived in Southampton, hopeful and starving, she'd found that her mathematical talent extended to identifying the ships flying in and out of the Spaceport, scanning the arc of their flights in a heartbeat, gauging velocity and lift, and guessing at their destinations.

If she couldn't get to the stars, at least she could image others traveling there, and watch them go.

Diana swallowed, aware of the tight clutch of hunger in her belly. Without a word, she pulled out the stale half loaf and hard cheese she'd been saving. Whatever Tipper was up to, it was better to at least take the edge off before they went.

When the sky was quiet, she asked again. "What did you find?"

"The passage—I'm sure of it!" Excitement shone in his eyes.

She finished chewing the last of the bread, then rose and rolled up her blanket, her thoughts spinning. Surely Tipper hadn't discovered a way into the Spaceport?

Despite herself, she found her heartbeat spinning faster with hope.

"Where?" she asked.

He glanced about, eyes sparkling, then lowered his voice. "Hidden in a building near the wall. We'll get into the spaceport today, Di. For true."

She couldn't believe it, not really. Tipper had "found" a passageway once before, that had only ended up connecting to the sewers. Still, she tucked her blanket away into the satchel where she kept her few possessions, then shoved the bag beneath a fall of rubble.

"Tally-ho, then," she said. Maybe, just maybe, their luck was about to change.

And it wasn't as though they had any other options.

CHAPTER 9

Darting like a mongoose, Tipper led her through the twists of the alleys, through falling-down buildings and past heaps of rubble, until they reached the sheer, shiny wall of the spaceport. It rose a dozen meters into the air, silvery and impermeable, and so clean.

Diana laid her hand against the surface, the alien material faintly cool against her palm. There was no need for a stun current—the Yxleti-made wall was impervious to any human effort. No knife or gun, laser or explosive could even mar it, let alone break through.

Nothing stood close to it. The few attempts people had made in the past to build their way over the wall had always met with destruction. Spaceport Security scanned the perimeter every morning and evening to ensure nothing was being built too close to their precious wall.

There were only two ways into the oval-shaped spaceport district, and both had airtight security. Passengers and those with official business used the front entrance at one end of the oval. Cargo and employees went through the

Spaceport Authority processing area on the other end. Between the two, nothing but high, sheer walls.

"Psst." Tipper waved at her from a shadowy ruin some distance away.

Diana joined him inside the run-down building, and he gave her a wide grin.

"Lookit this." He nudged a crumbling piece of pressboard aside with his foot to reveal a dark shaft disappearing into the ground.

She leaned over and peered into the blackness. The edges were perfectly straight, the hole just big enough to admit a body. Provided that a person was not afraid of closed-in, dark places. She shivered.

"Where does it go?"

"I waited for you, to find out."

Diana shot him a look. It wasn't just the fondness they had for one another that had made him wait, but the sense of self-preservation every streetrat needed in order to survive. It would be sheer foolishness to disappear down that black shaft without anyone knowing where you'd gone, or waiting up above to pull you back up if necessary.

"You've got a rope?" She glanced around the ruin. The two partially standing walls didn't provide nearly enough cover for what they were about to do.

"Sure. And lights. And water and the last of my brat bars, just in case." He went to the corner and rummaged beneath a piss-scented tarp, emerging with the described items.

"You're well prepared." She shouldn't be surprised, though. After all, this had been Tipper's dream for as long as she'd known him.

"'Course I am. Been saving things since forever. Here." He held out one of the foil-wrapped bars.

She shook her head. "I still have one from last night—at the station."

In her opinion, one was more than enough. B-rations, brats for short, were the lowest-level foodstuffs. Even at her hungriest, she could barely choke down a mouthful of the gluey substance. If it came to that, maybe rats would taste better.

"Nob," Tipper said, correctly interpreting her look of distaste.

"Ain't."

She wasn't a noble, despite those hazy memories of silky dresses and mathematics lessons and a puppy of her own. That was half a lifetime ago, or more. It didn't matter now. She patted the brat bar tucked into her trouser pocket, planning to give it to Tipper after they… well. After they found whatever it was they were going to find down there.

"Probably just leads to the sewers," she said, taking a sniff of the air over the shaft.

It wasn't as foul as she expected. Dry, not rank, with a whiff of fuel. A jagged shard of hope sawed through her. Could it actually be a tunnel into the spaceport?

Rumor was the Yxleti had used a network of tunnels when constructing the port. But they all had been filled up again, long ago. Even if this was a former passage to the spaceport, it surely ended in an impassable wall of rubble.

Still, her heart raced with possibility.

She helped Tipper secure the rope to the sturdiest beam they could find. He wrapped it around his chest and under his arms, then donned a pair of stained leather gloves two sizes too big.

"Are you sure you want to go first?" She glanced into the hole. "It looks deep."

"I found it, I get to explore it first. And I dropped a lightstick down there yesterday. Bottom's not too far."

He grinned at her. She had the feeling "not too far" had a different meaning, once you were dangling at the end of a rope.

"Speaking of light..." He held a battered lightstick out to her, then tucked a second one into a makeshift head-band and settled it over his filthy hair.

Before she could wish him luck, he scrambled over the edge of the shaft and let himself down.

Diana knelt and watched him go down. The shaft was small enough that he could brace his legs and back on opposite sides and control his descent. Once, he slipped, and she swallowed back a cry of dismay as he slid a full meter down the hole before catching himself.

Sooner than she would have liked, all she could see was the lightstick attached to his head. It bobbed up and down, sparking dull reflections from the sides of the shaft. After a while, the light stopped, and the rope jiggled wildly.

"Tipper?" She leaned over the hole, fear clenching her gut.

The rope went slack.

Something was down there, and had eaten him.

Dammit. Without comm devices—which no streetrat could ever afford—she had to guess at what was happening.

Hands shaking, she hauled the dangling rope back up and inspected the end. No blood, no fraying.

"Di." Tipper's voice echoed softly up.

She blew the stale air of fear out of her lungs. "Now what?" she hissed down into the hole.

"Going to explore. Sit tight."

The roar of ascent washed over the silvery spaceport walls. Diana glanced up as the Volux V-class freighter lumbered up into the lower atmosphere. Bound in-system, she'd guess; one of the outlying Jupiterean moons, or maybe just Mars.

"Tipper?" She leaned forward at the flicker of light from below.

"Di! Come down—it's a passage through."

She didn't believe it, though Tipper had never been a practical joker like some of the other streetrats.

"Who'll guard the rope?"

"I don't care." His voice was jubilant. "Hurry."

She tied the rope around her torso, hoping the knots would hold. Unlike Tipper, she hadn't brought gloves to protect her hands. It wasn't so far down that she'd burn her hands terribly—unless she fell.

Diana gave the rope a couple tugs, testing the beam. Solid enough. Gritting her teeth, she lowered herself into the shaft. The coarse hemp bit her palms, and the metal wall was cool against her back. Slowly, she inched down, the pale blue sky overhead becoming a smaller rectangle as the dark swallowed her. The only thing that made it bearable was knowing that Tipper and his lightstick were waiting for her at the bottom.

At last she saw the glow from below.

"The shaft ends," Tipper said. "There's a drop of a few meters to the floor."

Jaw aching from clenching her teeth, Diana's feet hit empty air. She kicked out, the rope slipping too quickly between her hands, and she hit the unyielding surface below. Her legs folded under her and she sat down, hard, on the floor of the tunnel.

"All right?" Tipper gave her a hand up.

"Well enough."

She straightened and gave an experimental stretch side to side. Other than what would probably be a spectacular bruise on her tailbone, and the rope burns on her palms, she was uninjured. She pulled the extra lightstick out of her pocket and flicked it on.

The straight, dim corridor was nothing special—except for the immense possibility it represented. Feeling a smile stretch her face, she nodded at Tipper.

"Lead on, sir."

They walked quickly, excitement pushing their pace. Despite that, Diana was still cautious, ticking off their steps in her head. When they were almost to the spot where the boundary wall stretched overhead, she held out her arm, halting Tipper.

"Wait," she said. "Did you come this far, earlier?"

"No." He bounced up and down on his toes. "Just far enough to see the passage was open."

She studied the corridor ahead. It looked safe, but stun currents were invisible until triggered. No streetrat traveled without an assortment of useful items in their pockets. Never knew when one might need a bit of string or graphite. Or, in this case, a pebble.

Diana tossed the stone a few meters ahead of them. It flew past the potential hazard point and kept going to clatter down on the floor. Nothing flared or buzzed.

"Safe enough." She hoped.

"Milady." Tipper swept out his hand in a move worthy of a gentleman.

"Coward," she murmured as she strode past him, winking to show she didn't truly mean it. He'd been first down into the darkness, after all.

She flinched, just a little, as she passed the boundary, but like the pebble, she passed through untouched. Tipper came up behind her. Their twin lightsticks reflected eerily off the silver walls, the pale yellow glow barely pushing back the blackness. They walked ten paces beyond the wall, then twenty.

"Why do you think they built this tunnel?" Tipper whispered.

She shrugged. Who knew why the enigmatic Yxleti did anything?

A hundred years ago they had appeared from the sky, crowned Victoria *Queen Eternal*, then stood back. They had allowed humans to use their strange technology to reach the stars, and they never interfered. Only watched.

Some scholars believed the Yxleti wanted to bring stability and prosperity to the human race, like some kind of benevolent overlords. Others argued that the aliens saw humans as an experiment, like creatures under a microscope, or in a zoo.

Whatever it was, nobody knew the answer, and the British Empire continued to spread into the galaxy without encountering any other sentient species.

"Well." Tipper held his light up, illuminating the sheer wall in front of them where the tunnel ended. "Now what?"

"Go back for the rope?" She leaned back, lifting her lightstick high. "I think there's a trapdoor overhead."

"How do we get to it? Hidden ladders or something?"

That made sense. The workers who used this tunnel in the past wouldn't want to be carrying around ladders as they went about their business.

"Take that side." She nodded to the left, then moved to the right and started running her hands over the smooth wall. Soon, her fingers found an irregularity—a long seam running vertically up from the floor to the ceiling.

"Here," she said, pulling out her makeshift dagger.

Tipper hurried to her side, and together they pried and pulled at the metal. Diana levered it up, then Tipper wedged his gloved hand in the space and yanked. Finally, with a loud creak, the seam parted to reveal a ladder built against the wall.

She jumped back, dropping her lightstick, but Tipper just stood there, laughing. Her heart looped in spirals of astonished joy as she stared at the ladder ascending the wall. They'd done it! They'd actually found their way into the spaceport.

Well, almost. Whether or not they could actually get inside remained to be seen.

DIANA LET TIPPER GO FIRST UP THE METAL LADDER, THEN followed a safe distance behind. The rungs were cool as rain under her fingers. As they neared the ceiling of the corridor, strange, thumping vibrations filled the air. At first she thought it was drums, but the rhythm was too uneven.

"Footsteps." She reached up and tapped Tipper on the leg. "I think this opens onto a walkway."

That complicated matters. Spaceport travelers would not stand idly by as two streetrats clambered up from a shaft in the floor. Especially not two individuals as soiled and bedraggled as herself and Tipper. Her last visit to the bathhouse had been nearly a fortnight ago, and who knew how long it had been since Tipper had washed? Years, maybe, judging by his rank boy-sweat odor and matted hair.

"Let's get closer," he said. "I think I see a bolt across."

Despite her doubts that the hatch was secured by anything so mundane as a bolt, it turned out he was right.

She gripped the sides of the ladder tightly as he slid the bolt back in slow, screeching increments. Hopefully, the people tromping above would pay little mind to the noise.

Tipper braced his palms against the trapdoor.

She grabbed the ragged edge of his trousers. "Wait. Not yet."

She'd been counting the steps, the ebb and flow, the pattern swirling in her head in elliptical shapes. A rise, a smoothening, a dip as the traffic diminished. She didn't think there would be a perfect moment for them to emerge, not in the middle of the afternoon at the busy spaceport, but a good opportunity was coming. Soon, soon.

"Now," she said. "Quick!"

Tipper heaved the hatch open and flung himself out. She was right behind him. The door banged against the floor, and the three people in evidence turned, staring. One, a woman in a long, ruffled gown, began to scream.

Moving in accord, Diana and Tipper flipped the hatch closed and raced away, deeper into the spaceport. The woman's shrieks echoed behind them. Unlike the alleyways of Southampton, there were no side passages, no dark places to duck into. Just flat, straight walls. Diana's breath burned in her chest, her eyes darting from side to side, barely registering the looks of shock as she and Tipper dashed past.

They had to find a hiding place. Behind them, she could hear the rough commands of Spaceport Security, ordering people out of the way. Her blood iced as she considered the very real possibility that she and Tipper might get shot.

Oh, why hadn't they waited until night, when the

chance of discovery was much lower? They were fools, the both of them, carried along by the current of excitement without considering the cost.

"Stop!" a deep voice bellowed. "Stop those two!"

Diana sidestepped a man in a bowler hat, then wrenched out of an older lady's grasp. The wild exhilaration of breaching the spaceport had curdled to panic. She and Tipper were in trouble deep.

"Hey!" Tipper yelped.

She whirled to see him caught, arms pinned against his side by a tall man in a tweed suit.

"Tip!"

She went to pull him from his captor's grasp, but those few seconds was all it took for security to catch up to them. Before she could dash away, a woman in a bright blue uniform grabbed her wrist and slapped a shackle on it. The man holding Tipper thrust him into another guard's custody, and, just like that, their mad adventure was at an end.

Her euphoria was gone, replaced by a looming sense of dread.

A quick, impersonal frisking left the guard holding Diana's makeshift knife and her unwanted brat bar. She'd missed the money bound to the inside of Diana's ankle, though—not that tuppence and three was worth anything, where they were going.

Jail, most like—but Diana hoped rather desperately that she and Tip wouldn't be separated. Surely their crime wasn't enough to warrant transportation? The thought made her stomach clench.

"It's over, you two," the guard holding her said. "Come quietly."

Diana pulled in a deep breath. At least she'd seen the inside of the spaceport—however briefly. She didn't try to pull away. Though she'd never been in stun shackles before, she knew how they worked and had no desire to put them, or the guard's temper, to the test.

Tipper shuffled his feet and hung his head low—no doubt remembering his all-to-recent captivity—but Diana looked everywhere. They'd paid dearly enough to get inside the spaceport, and she wanted to take it all in: the travelers hurrying to catch their ships, porters pushing brass luggage trollies behind, the uniformed starliner attendants, a woman clad in brown leather, who surely must be a pilot.

And stitched through it all, the thrum of ships decelerating, landing, taking off. The air vibrated with the sound. Windows on the far wall showed tantalizing glimpses of the ships outside, but Diana knew better than to linger.

The officers led them down one shining hallway, then another. Ahead, doors whooshed open and closed, the brighter light of day spilling through.

And then they were outside, on a partially enclosed walkway, and Diana nearly forgot she was a prisoner. On the right-hand side of the walk, ships spread in a half-circle in their berths. She couldn't help but slow down as she stared, cataloguing. There—a Xeros 2000, sleek as an arrow. Beside it, the crablike shell of an older hauler bound for the asteroid mining belt.

On the far left, another freighter rose, engines wheezing, but holding. Overloaded, by the way it listed slightly in the air, and not with legal goods she'd wager. She frowned. Couldn't the authorities tell when smugglers freighted contraband out right under their noses?

At the midpoint of the freighter's arc, a Class A Cruzline ship began ignition. The fore engines fired, and then the aft. Slowly, the ship rose, gleaming and no doubt full of important and moneyed passengers.

Diana halted. Something was wrong.

"Keep moving," the guard said. Her name badge simply read *Nails*.

"Wait… wait." Diana leaned forward, listening, watching, calculating the arc of the Cruzline as it began its ascent.

Deep in her memory, she heard the shriek of an omnibus horn. Felt her blood slow as she once again recognized the trajectory of disaster. This time, they *must* listen.

"Stop that ship!" She lifted her shackled wrist and pointed at the sleek passenger ship.

The woman's hand fell to the stun unit at her belt. "Don't make me use this."

"They're going to crash!" Diana strained forward. "Contact the control center—it's a direct collision course in… twenty seconds. Please, tell them! Please!"

The guard narrowed her eyes, but the panic in Diana's voice must have convinced her. Her gaze went unfocused as she activated her nano-comm and spoke hurriedly, using lots of acronyms and letters.

Twelve seconds.

"Do it," the security woman said, her voice hard. "I don't care—just abort the liftoff."

Diana's attention fixed on the gruesome calculation unfolding overhead. Her lungs clenched so tight, she had no room for breath. *No air. I'm sorry, Mama. Papa.*

The bright ship tried to veer, but it was going fast. Too fast.

Eight seconds. Seven. Six.

The Cruzline's engines stalled, and Diana sucked in her breath. Three. Two.

One.

The edge of the Cruzline nicked the freighter, then spun out, but beautifully slowly. The pilot was good enough to control the move, steering his craft into a shining silver loop. The freighter wobbled, the collision barley nudging the massive ship off-course.

Diana grasped the railing to keep herself upright, her knees weak with relief. With redemption. The breath shuddered back into her lungs as the Cruzline steadied and returned to its berth. A security bugship, lights flashing, buzzed the freighter, leading it back to the customs screening pad.

Eyes blurred, she glanced up at the cloud-specked blue overhead. In a different universe, the air would be full of fire and death and a hundred personal tragedies. But not this world. Not this day.

She lifted her hand to rub at her eyes, the motion cut short by the cuff on her wrist. With a slump of her shoulders, she turned back to the guard. For a moment, she'd forgotten that she was still a prisoner, bound for more trouble than she'd ever imagined.

"Right away, sir," Nails said. Her gaze cleared and she looked at Diana. "Taking you upstairs to meet the director."

Diana glanced at Tipper, who stood uncharacteristically silent. If they were separated, she had the feeling she'd never see him again.

"My companion comes, too," she said.

The security guard hesitated.

"I mean it." Diana put the steel of truth in her voice. She hadn't spent her entire savings just to see him hauled away by Spaceport Security.

Whatever was going on—and it probably had to do with the averted crash—she and Tipper were in it together. After all, without him, she wouldn't even have been there to witness the near-collision.

"Very well—the both of you. Don't try anything." This last was directed at Tipper, with a narrow-eyed glare.

He put on his wounded face, and Diana felt a stir of grim amusement. His expression wouldn't get him anywhere with Nails, but at least they wouldn't be separated.

The security guards led them through several corridors, and then to a grav lift tucked in a corner. Another guard stood there, clearly expecting them. He keyed open the lift, and the doors swooshed open.

Nails led her inside, and Diana tried not to show the nerves etching a jagged graph through her mind. It was too posh—the marble floor and polished wooden walls of the lift far above the normal trappings of the spaceport. The smooth, fast rise left her courage sinking to her feet. Tipper shot her a look that showed too much eye, clearly just as nervous about wherever they were going.

The lift slowed and halted, the doors slid open, and Diana blinked at the view. She barely noticed the plush burgundy carpeting and wingback chairs, the wide desk or the gray-haired man sitting behind it. Her eyes were drawn inexorably to the huge bank of windows on the wall opposite the lift.

They were at the very top of the spaceport. Ships dived and flew, and she could see the neighborhoods of Southampton spread out beyond the silvery wall. The portside slums, of course, were behind them—a view no one wanted to contemplate.

"And so." The man behind the desk stood, revealing a portly figure dressed in well-tailored clothing. "Our heroine of the hour. Come, come."

He gestured to her, and Diana took a step forward, trying not to wince at the pain in her tailbone.

"Wait." He held up a hand. "Remove her cuff, Nails, if you please. I would like to shake this young woman's hand without fear of a shock."

He laughed, and the security guards guffawed along with him, though their laughter sounded forced.

"Apologies, Director Quinn." Nails quickly took the cuff off, with a warning look at Diana. Her hand grazed the lightpistol holstered at her side, the message clear.

The luxurious surroundings made Diana acutely aware of her own grime and stink. She lifted her chin. If this director fellow wanted to talk to her, he'd have to take her as she was.

Somewhat to her surprise, he actually did step forward and take her hand, giving it a firm shake.

"What is your name?" he asked.

"Diana." She didn't think he'd appreciate her street name of Diver. "Diana Smythe."

"The spaceport owes you a debt of thanks, Miss Smythe. Are you aware that a very important delegation was aboard that Cruzline vessel?"

She shook her head, but it didn't surprise her. Who else but the toffest nobs would book passage on that kind of ship?

"Without your acute observational skills, a very messy incident would have occurred. Tell me—how did you know the ships were on a collision course?"

"It was clear as glass, least to me," she said. "The liftoff arcs intersected. That freighter's smuggling something. They were too slow to clear the line of flight." When Nails prodded her in the back, she added a belated, "Sir."

"And you could tell all that at a glance?" He didn't sound doubtful, just curious.

"Yes."

"She's always been good at such things, sir," Tipper said. "Knowing how a mark moves through a crowd, or the fall of dice, or—"

He broke off as Diana elbowed him in the ribs.

"I notice suchlike," she said.

"Hm." Director Quinn gave her a keen look. "Join me at the window, if you would."

Diana followed him to the expanse, and her spirits lifted at the view. The whole port spread out below her feet. All those lives and dreams and arrows to the stars, shot right from here—the busiest port in England, the center of Empire—straight into the heart of the stars.

"What do you see?" he asked. "Describe the ships to me as they come and go."

It was a test, though she wasn't sure what the penalty

for failure might be. She narrowed her eyes and rolled forward on the balls of her feet, focusing on the geometry, the arcs and parabolas forming and re-forming outside the window.

"That ship—the Tellium X class, just landing. They're coming in a little too fast. Bet they get a warning. And the Aristo there needs a tune-up. They should have better lift, especially a later model like that."

She continued to scan the spaceport, pointing out holes where ships were too slow or too fast, speculating aloud on destinations and cargo, flagging possible smugglers and lazy pilots. All the while, the director nodded and, judging by his slightly unfocused stare, accessed his nano-comm.

Ten minutes passed, then twenty. Diana's throat tightened from talking so much. Behind her, she could hear Tipper fidgeting and coughing. Finally, the director spoke.

"Impressive," he said. "You have quite a gift, Miss Smythe. You strike me as something along the lines of a mathematical genius. Have you ever considered putting your talents to official use?"

She took a step back, her dingy boots sinking into the plush carpet. Did they mean to barter? No jail time for her and Tipper, in exchange for her servitude? Or could she ask for even more? With the director praising her odd skills, perhaps she had the advantage.

It was a daring notion, but then, the day had been full of extraordinary things. And she'd just saved two ships full of people, after all. That was worth something.

"Seems to me you need me in your employ, then," she said. "After stopping the crash and all."

Director Quinn's brows rose. "Do you think so?"

"Who else could spot the things I just saw? The space-port would function more efficiently if you hired me. I could help watch the ships, calculate trajectories, tell when something's off. Don't you need something like that?"

"As a matter of fact, we do. Which is why we've commissioned work on a Calculations Device that would do the very things you mention."

Her heart dipped. They didn't need her then, and it would be jail after all.

"However," the director said, "work on the device is going rather slowly. Until it's functional, I don't see why you couldn't join us here in the spaceport. Under proper supervision, of course."

"Then you'll do it?" She tried not to let her hope show in her eyes. "You'll hire me on?"

He frowned. "It wouldn't do to have a streetrat in our employ. Would you be willing to live in a flat provided by the spaceport, in addition to your salary?"

"I don't live in the West Quay slums because I love it," she said, perhaps a bit too tartly.

Director Quinn simply laughed, however. "I'll take that as a yes, then. Miss Smythe, on behalf of Spaceport Authority, I would like to offer you employment. Help us achieve the stars to the best of our ability, and put your rare skills in the service of the greater cause of humanity."

It was a pompous speech, but it stirred her all the same. There was a glint of truth in the director's eye that touched her, even more than his grand words. Who didn't dream of the freedom of the galaxy, after all?

"Tipper comes with me," she said. After what they'd

been through, she couldn't just abandon him to his fate. "What's the pay?"

"Ever practical, aren't you?" He named a sum that stilled her heart for a moment.

But only a moment.

"A week?" she asked, half in jest.

This time it was Director Quinn's turn to blink. Then he laughed again.

"And why not? Do we have an agreement?"

She pulled in a breath and glanced once more at the spinning arcs and cosines weaving outside the window. The sum she'd named would keep her in grand style. Even better, it would give Tipper, and any other streetrat who wanted out, a ticket to the stars. And herself as well, when she was ready to go.

Slowly, she gazed up, past the blue, to where the galaxy gleamed and shone. That was her ultimate dream. But working at the spaceport was a long sight better than sleeping in the West Quay gutters, with no way out.

She extended a grimy hand to the director, and smiled when he again took it without hesitation.

"Yes, sir," she said. "We surely do."

CHAPTER 11

THE NEXT HOUR WAS SPENT RATHER UNGLAMOROUSLY IN filling out paperwork. The director's secretary raised one slender eyebrow when Diana signed her name, and she wondered if he was impressed with her penmanship or thought it rather childish.

Not that she cared what he—or anyone—thought of her. Director Quinn approved, and that was all that mattered.

Nails took Tipper along with her to fetch them all something to eat and returned with several packets of fish and chips. The oily smell permeated the luxurious suite, but somehow didn't seem out of place. Diana and Tipper were permitted a few quiet moments alone at a table tucked into a back alcove.

"What's next?" Tipper asked, devouring his chips at an alarming rate. "Are they giving you a place to live? When do you start work? What—"

"Just don't choke on your food, and I'll answer every-thing," she said. "Yes, I'm getting a flat in one of the buildings the spaceport owns, though I have to pay rent. Don't look so unhappy, Tip. I can afford it."

It was an astonishing phrase, and she repeated it silently in her head a few times, savoring the words. *I can afford it.*

Of course, she wasn't planning on spending her money like it was water. But still, what a glorious feeling.

"Also," she continued, "there's room for you. If you like."

He paused, a piece of fish halfway to his mouth. "For true, Di? You'd take me in?"

"Of course. We wouldn't be here if you hadn't found that tunnel." Which was probably already filled in, barricaded against any more riffraff finding their way in. "But I do have one condition." She gave him a stern look. "Regular baths."

He blinked at her, then popped the fish in his mouth and chewed noisily.

"I s'pose I could do that," he said.

She leaned forward. "And no more stealing—for either of us. We're off the streets for good, Tip."

"What'll I do, then?"

"School?"

He shook his head vigorously. "I know plenty, already."

"Then an apprenticeship, maybe. And a tutor, so that you can polish up your reading and writing." *I can afford it.* She didn't think she'd ever tire of that phrase.

"Maybe I can get work," he said. "At a fish and chips stand. That'd be fine, wouldn't it?"

"It would, indeed."

"Miss Smythe," the director called. "If you're finished with your supper, we have a few more details to go over."

"Here." She pushed the last of her chips to Tipper. "Stay here. I should be done soon with all this. And then they'll take us over to our new flat."

It was a dizzying thought. Indeed, it had been a dizzying day altogether—and a bit frightening how quickly everything was happening.

"Here's your temporary ID badge," the director said when she rejoined him. He slid a card across the desk to her. "We'll take a more permanent holo-photo when you're ready."

It was a polite way of saying "when you've gotten yourself cleaned up," but she couldn't begrudge him. She could do with a clean face and combed hair, and clothing that wasn't falling apart at the seams.

"In addition," he continued, laying a thick envelope on the desk before her, "this contains two keys to your new flat, and an advance on your salary. Perhaps you'd like to do some clothes shopping."

Despite the mildness of his tone, it was a clear order. Not that she disagreed. She was no longer Diver, the stree-trat, but Miss Diana Smythe. Not quite the young lady of Quality she barely remembered from her past, but there was no denying she'd come up in the world. A much-mended shirt and boy's trousers simply wouldn't do.

"Thank you." She glanced at the blue-uniformed guard standing at the door. "Is there a certain dress code, sir?"

He gave her a thoughtful look. "Professional, I'd think. Skirts, but not too wide. No nano-lifters, of course. Long sleeves."

"Hair up," the secretary said from his desk at the front of the room. "No ankles showing."

The secretary's name, she'd learned over the course of the afternoon, was Le. She wasn't sure if it was his first or last name, however, and was a little afraid to ask. The man clearly disapproved of her.

"You may have the morning off tomorrow," Director Quinn said. "Do some shopping, get settled in. Report at one pm to the downstairs lift. Nails will meet you and escort you up."

Clearly Diana wasn't going to be trusted with the codes to the top of the spaceport. Just as well—if anything ever happened, she couldn't be blamed.

He beckoned the security guard over. "Speaking of escorts, Nails will take you through the back gate now, and up to Queensway—the neighborhood where your flat is located. It's furnished. Apartment 54, I believe, in the Queensway Tower."

"Thank you, sir," she said, picking up the envelope. It was thick with bills, the metal lumps of the keys bumpy beneath her fingers.

Tipper jumped up from the table and wiped his mouth on the back of his sleeve.

"Right then," he said, his eyes bright. He made a low, extravagant bow to the director.

Nails let out a snort, either of disapproval or laughter. Maybe both. It was clear to Diana that the guard was trying hard not to be taken with Tipper, but for all his flaws, he was a sweet boy.

"Come on, you two," Nails said, jerking her head toward the silver doors of the lift.

Tip scampered ahead, but Diana turned to the director

and gave him the best curtsy she could manage, considering her trousers and generally disheveled state.

"I'm indebted to you," she said.

"Oh, we'll work you hard, never fear." He gave her a genial smile. "Until tomorrow, Miss Smythe."

She turned and followed Nails, keeping her chin high and her stride confident as they went past Le's station. Diana imagined she could feel a chilly circle surrounding his desk, but she didn't glance his way. He'd realize soon enough that she was no threat to him and his work.

Once inside the lift, Tipper gave her a greasy-chinned grin.

"Can you believe it, Di? A flat of our own, and spending money!"

She weighed the envelope in her hands, heavy with promise. No, she couldn't quite fathom it, even as she tucked the bills and keys safely out of sight under her shirt.

As Nails escorted them out of the spaceport and onto the train packed with commuters, Diana held her breath. Surely she was dreaming. At any moment she'd wake, wrapped in her hole-filled blanket, the last of the night's fog hazing the streets and hunger clamping her belly.

At the third stop up the line, they disembarked. The station was busy; people flowing back and forth from the train platforms while a large clock ticked away the minutes above the arched entrance. Tipper craned his neck and flexed his fingers, no doubt ready to dip into some of the rich pockets passing by.

"Tip," Diana said warningly and grabbed his hand for good measure.

His fingers were warm and oily, and he shot her a wounded look. "I wasn't."

She raised a brow at him. Habits died hard. She couldn't deny that she was calculating the crowd, fixing the location of the likeliest marks in her mind, plotting a course to intersect. But that was a certain path to ruin.

"We can't spoil this," she said. "Everything on the up and up from here on out."

"Aye," Nails said, giving them both a narrow-eyed look. "And don't you forget it. We'll be watching you."

Tipper let out a sigh, but kept holding Diana's hand as they followed the guard out of the station. Two-story red brick town houses lined the street, interspersed with small shops and pubs. Trees stretched overhead, sending dappled shade onto the cobblestones, where steam-powered vehicles and horse-drawn carts passed.

She dimly remembered walking like this, one arm stretched out, clasping hands with her older sister and feeling… safe.

Of course, life wasn't safe. Everything could change in a heartbeat—and did. But for now, the sun had come out and the taste of freedom was like strong ale, bubbling through her and making her giddy.

"Queensway Tower," Nails said, indicating the tall structure ahead.

It was aptly named, rising six stories above the surrounding buildings, windows catching the lowering sun and reflecting it back a hundredfold, until it seemed the whole tower was filled with light.

Beside her, Tipper pulled in an awed breath as they strode up to the entryway. The fan window above the door and gilded plaster archway resonated faintly with Diana, a dim echo of the grandeur of her past.

"Keys?" Nails asked, folding her arms.

Belatedly, Diana pulled the envelope out of her shirt and fished out the two keys: heavy brass, with long stems and notched teeth at the far end. Ceremoniously, she handed one to Tipper.

"Don't lose it," she said.

He rolled his eyes. "I could pick this lock in under a minute."

"Actually, you couldn't." Nails gave him an arch look. "There are signature nanos embedded in the metal. Anything lacking that signature that's inserted into the keyhole will set off alarms."

"Oh." Tipper looked down at the key in his grubby palm, and then folded his fingers over it.

Feeling like she was opening the door to a treasure room, Diana put her key into the lock. It turned, smooth as butter, and with a click, the door unlatched. A waft of flower-scented air escaped as Nails pulled the door open.

A vase of striped lilies sat on a table in the center of the marble-floored foyer. A tiled pattern marched around the edge, and Diana was glad to see that all the pieces lined up uniformly. She wouldn't have to set her teeth and ignore the pattern whenever she entered or left the building.

"The lift's over here." Nails led them around the table to the far corner. "I'm authorized to set the keypad to you."

She tinkered with the pad, then beckoned Diana to place her thumb on the surface. A light swept across the keypad, followed by a single chime.

"Right. You're done." The guard nodded to Tipper. "Your turn."

Tipper complied, then glanced around the foyer. "Bet there's all kinda monitoring devices in here."

"You'd be right on that score." Nails shot him a look. "And don't forget it."

"Yes, ma'am." Tipper saluted, and Diana dipped her head to hide her smile.

"Streetrats." Nails shook her head, but her lips twitched ever so slightly with amusement. "Up we go. Fifth floor."

"All the way up?" Tipper's eyes widened. "That's posh."

Diana had the feeling that the apartment would dumbfound him entirely. And probably her too, for that matter. She did the honors, setting her thumb on the keypad to summon the lift. In a matter of moments they were whooshing up to the top story.

The lift dinged open to reveal yet another foyer, this one floored in warm parquet wood. Two doors led off to the right, two to the left.

"There are four apartments on each level," Nails said. "Don't be troublesome neighbors, understand?"

""Course we won't," Tipper said, with his most innocent expression.

Diana nodded, catching the warning look in the guard's eye. It was up to her to keep Tipper out of trouble. She'd need to find something for him to do as soon as possible, or he'd get up to mischief before she could even turn around.

She let out a quiet sigh. Already the expectations of her new life were folding around her, pushing her in directions she wasn't entirely certain she wanted to go. Caring for another person was dangerous. And despite her brave words, she'd just taken on a job she wasn't sure she could perform to the director's satisfaction.

Still better than the streets, she reminded herself. A thousand times better.

"You can use the same key as downstairs," Nails said, gesturing to the door in the right hand corner, marked *54*. "Each apartment's key opens the building, but is warded to only work for their own unit."

Diana glanced down, seeing a little star cutout centered on the key's teeth. Her hand trembling slightly, she turned the key in the lock of her new home.

CHAPTER 12

THE DOOR SWUNG OPEN TO REVEAL A BRIGHTLY LIT SITTING room with large windows looking out over the city. A Turkish carpet in rich red and gold covered the floor and, as promised, there was furniture: a sofa richly upholstered in velvet and brocade, the wooden arms of the chairs polished to a satin shine, plump cushions decorating the settee.

There was artwork, too—landscapes in gold frames, and a jade urn filled with more lilies.

Blinking, Diana stepped inside.

"Criminy," Tipper said under his breath as he followed.

"There's a water closet to the left, there, and a bathing room," Nails said. "The kitchen's just beyond. Two bedrooms across the hall."

Although Diana knew the flat was small by the standards of the gentry, it felt like a palace. Like a soap bubble illusion that could pop at any time. Cautiously, she went over to the tall windows, careful not to touch the white curtains with her grubby hands.

Southampton looked so orderly from above, the River Itchen sparkling along one edge. Church spires poked up into the air, and tidy green squares were scattered among the neighborhoods, edged with trees. It bore almost no resemblance to the city she knew.

To the far left, barely in view, lay the spaceport. Ships sparkled in the duskening air, handfuls of silver and gold flung out into the sky. Beyond the port was the smudge of the slums. She wondered if there was anything Tipper wanted to fetch from there.

For her part, she was happy to leave her broken comb and ragged blanket behind. There was nothing she wanted from the bowels of the port.

"The maids come in weekly, to do the laundry and cleaning," Nails said. "You're on your own for meals, though. Most residents here hire a cook, dine out, or eat takeaway."

Tipper went forward, eyes fixed on the kitchen. "I'd like to do some cooking."

"Don't burn the place down," Nails said. "Should I show you how to run the bath?"

It was an unsubtle reference to how grimy they were, but Diana didn't blame the guard. It was true that she and Tipper were downright filthy. So much so that it felt like the very act of their breathing was soiling the pristine flat.

"Come on, Tip," she said. "We'll clean up, then explore the rest."

"Excellent choice," Nails said. "I believe there are spare dressing gowns in the linen closet."

"How do you know so much about this place?" Tipper

asked, retreating from the bright lure of the kitchen. "Do you stay here?"

"Me?" Nails gave a short laugh. "No, I've my own place closer to the river. Truth is, I used to be in service here, before I took the training to become a security guard. Spaceport Security patrols this building, too, so I'm back from time to time."

"Grand, then we'll see you about," Tipper said, genuine gladness in his voice.

Nails scowled at him. "You'll see me more than that, if you don't behave."

Tipper only winked in reply and led the way to the bathing room.

The room held a good sized tub, Diana was happy to see. No more trips to the Turkish baths across the river. Nails showed them where the soap and towels were kept, and how to regulate the water temperature, then took her leave.

"I'll check on you in a few days," she said as Diana went with her to the sitting room, leaving Tip to run the water in the bath. "Make sure you're keeping out of trouble."

And not ruining the flat, Diana assumed.

"Won't I see you at the spaceport?" she asked.

"Here and there." Nails shrugged and pulled open the front door. "Keep that boy busy, as best you can."

"I will." Diana hoped, anyway.

"There's a handheld you can use, in the far bedroom. Good luck."

Before Diana could thank Nails, the guard slipped out and pulled the door closed behind her. The sound of running water and the smell of orange blossom soap filled the flat.

"Don't let it flood," Diana called. "When you get in the tub, the water will rise."

"I know that!" Despite the confidence in his voice, Tipper shut the water off immediately.

She paused outside the bathing room door. "Would you like help?"

"I'm not a baby."

"Well, don't drown. And don't just pretend to bathe, either."

She heard a snort of derision. Smiling to herself, she moved on into the kitchen. It was well stocked with dishes and an assortment of gadgets, most of which she didn't have the faintest idea how to use. To her surprise, one of the cupboards held a few food items: cooking oil, spices. Nothing she could make a meal of, however.

There was a dishcloth beside the sink. She wetted it and removed the smudges her fingers had left on the white cabinets during her explorations. While she was at the sink, she washed her hands. Brown water flowed down the drain, and it took a rather long time until it ran clear.

Before she went into the tub, she'd rinse off, like they did at the Turkish baths. No use sitting in water scummed with her own grime.

The bedrooms were as bright and airy as the rest of the flat, though one was certainly smaller. That one would be Tipper's. Her room, at the back corner, held another spectacular view. For a while she simply stood there, hugging herself to prove that she was real. That all of it was real.

The sound of splashing and off-key singing drifted down the hall. She hoped Tipper remembered to wash his hair, too.

There were two doors on the far wall. She opened one to find a spacious closet. The other opened into an alcove holding a second commode and a small sink.

Such luxury.

For a moment she faltered, her throat tightening with fear. What if Director Quinn decided he'd made a mistake? What if she arrived at the spaceport on the morrow to find everything taken away again, as easily as it had been given?

Well then. She swallowed and squared her shoulders. At least she'd be cleaner than she was now—and a bit richer as well. She'd buy clothing for both of them, and a hearty breakfast, and then conceal the rest of the money about her person. Just in case.

"I'm done," Tipper announced, stepping out of the bathing room.

He was wearing one of the dressing gowns, and even with the sleeves rolled up, it was ridiculously overlarge. The sound of water glugging down the drain came from the bathing room, and his bare feet made damp marks on the golden wood.

"Well, look at that," Diana said, inspecting him. "Your hair is lighter than ever I thought. Not dark brown, at all."

He made a face at her. "Do I really have to wash it every time?"

"Yes," she said, knowing that he'd do no such thing. But as long as he didn't get too greasy, they could both pretend he was.

"You get the small bedroom," she said. "Don't make too much a mess of things while I'm bathing."

"'Course not."

Hoping he'd be true to his word, Diana went to take her bath.

CHAPTER 13

THE NEXT AFTERNOON, AT A QUARTER-TO-ONE, DIANA presented herself at the private lift leading to Director Quinn's office suite. Her new clothing felt stiff and strange; the boots tight about her feet, the bodice of her dark blue dress hugging her form, instead of disguising it. Diana fought the urge to slouch, and instead made herself march confidently through the shiny corridors of the spaceport.

No darting from corner to corner, no glancing back over her shoulder. Still, she couldn't help but calculate the movement of the crowd, idly noticing purses and pockets ripe for picking. A harried-looking matron shepherded two boisterous boys in front of her. Diana correctly interpreted their darting movements and nimbly slipped past, smiling to herself.

It wasn't as though her skills were going untapped, after all. The entire array of the spaceport was hers, hundreds of ships a day waiting for her to watch them go. It was an exhilarating thought.

She touched the crystal button she still wore beneath

her clothing, for luck. Instead of being threaded through a dirty bit of string, it now resided on a fine silver chain.

In addition, she wore a ring set with jewels that could be pried out, and had an ornate gold pocket watch pinned to her dress. All small items of value that could be easily sold, if it came to that.

She wore a corset, too. The woman at the shop had insisted that a young lady going about without a corset was practically naked. Diana hadn't argued too much, as the garment provided an excellent hiding place for her bank notes, especially if worn loosely cinched.

"Miss Smythe?" the guard at the lift said.

Diana was sorry to see it wasn't Nails. Well, perhaps tomorrow.

"Yes," she said, showing her temporary badge.

The guard nodded and keyed open the lift, then stood back to let her enter. Somewhat to her surprise, he didn't accompany her in.

Of course, she wasn't a prisoner wearing a stun cuff this time.

Keeping her chin high, Diana waited for the doors to close. No doubt there were hidden monitoring devices inside the lift. Probably all over the spaceport. She and Tipper had been quite deluded about not getting caught, but the excitement of it all had swept away her common sense.

And it had worked out for the best, hadn't it?

At least, she hoped so.

The door swooshed open at the top floor, and Diana stepped out. She swallowed past the fear drying her throat and nodded cordially to Le at his desk.

"Good afternoon," she said, hanging her hat and new umbrella on the nearby stand.

Gloves on, or off? It would be difficult to use her new handheld with them on, and besides, they were still so new. Better to keep them as clean as possible. She pulled them off and folded them carefully away into her reticule.

The secretary watched her, unblinking. "At least you've cleaned up well. The director is waiting for you in the conference room."

Lee pointed, and she followed his direction, trying to ignore the man's rudeness.

The conference room was furnished with a large wooden table polished to a high sheen and several leather-upholstered chairs, two of which were occupied. Director Quinn, at the head of the table, stood and greeted her with a smile as she stepped inside.

"Miss Smythe, welcome. I'd like you to meet your new colleague, Lord Atkinson."

He gestured to the man on his right, who had also risen. Lord Atkinson was a younger fellow with dark brown hair, sharp-faced, and very well dressed. A diamond stickpin sparkled from his blue silk necktie. The color of the cloth precisely matched his eyes, which Diana knew was no accident.

"Lord Atkinson," she said, dropping a curtsey. The move felt much more graceful when performed in skirts and petticoats rather than trousers.

"Miss Smythe, I'm delighted to make your acquaintance," he said in a voice as smooth and rich as dark honey.

Despite his cordial words, there was a faint edge in his tone—something Diana couldn't quite place. Probably just annoyance that he was being forced to be polite to a mere streetrat. The gentry were very particular about such things.

"Please, have a seat." The director gestured Diana to the chair across from Lord Atkinson. "Now that you're here, Le will bring us in some tea."

The men waited until she sat, before taking their seats, which she found amusing. If she wanted, she had the power to fuss about in her reticule and keep them standing an uncomfortably long time. But not today.

"Lord Atkinson is working on that exciting project I mentioned yesterday," the director said. "Perhaps you might explain it, my lord. You'll find that Miss Smythe will follow you quite well."

She sent Director Quinn a grateful glance. He, at least, seemed to hold her in some esteem.

Lord Atkinson's eyebrow went up, but he didn't hesitate to speak.

"I'm building a Calculations Device," he said. "Have you heard of Babbage's work?"

She tilted her head, rummaging about in her memory. The name sounded familiar, a far echo from her past, but she couldn't place it.

"I'm afraid not, my lord."

His smile was indulgent. "Of course. Well, he pioneered a machine called the Difference Engine, which could perform all kinds of rapid computations. Far faster than a human mind is capable of." This was accompanied by a rather pointed look.

Diana nodded. There was no use in trying to defend

herself. Most people didn't share her odd ability. Perhaps no one did.

"I am building upon Babbage's work," he continued, "and creating a device capable of tracking the ships as they come in and out of the spaceport. As you know, Director Quinn is very interested in finding ways to increase the efficiency and safety of operations here, at the gateway to the Empire."

"Yes." The director steepled his fingers and gave her a genial look. "I thought you and Lord Atkinson could collaborate. Your insights would be invaluable, and he might be inspired in different, more effective directions by watching your mind at work."

"My device is well on its way," Lord Atkinson said, a touch defensively. "And while Miss Smythe's input might be helpful, it's certainly not essential."

"Still," Director Quinn said, "I'm sure you'll find the workings of her mind to be well worth studying. And if your machine cannot fulfill the necessary requirements, then we are most fortunate to have Miss Smythe at hand to take its place."

Lord Atkinson scowled. "I assure you, I will be able to fulfill this commission."

"Let us hope so." The director paused as Le came into the room bearing a tea tray.

Diana feared she'd be asked to pour out, and embarrass herself by missing some crucial bit of etiquette, but it fell to the secretary to hand around the cups and saucers. A pure white tower of sugar cubes followed, and Diana carefully used the silver tongs to place a lump into her cup rather than the more expedient tool of her fingers.

She poured a dollop of milk in, too, then stirred. The clink of silver against porcelain sent up another echo of recognition. Surely her mother had taken tea like this, in a wallpapered room full of gossiping ladies.

Lee withdrew, and for a moment they all sipped their tea in silence.

"Then it's settled." Director Quinn set down his cup and beamed at her. "Lord Atkinson will observe you at work each morning, Miss Smythe, and hopefully apply what he learns to the completion of his new device. I'm certain it will be a most fruitful partnership."

"Certainly," she said. "I'll do my best."

Lord Atkinson smiled at her, though his eyes remained cold. "I look forward to it."

He did not sound pleased, however, but Diana didn't fret. As long as he wasn't outright hostile, she could manage perfectly well. A little animosity from Lord Atkinson was a thousand times better than a beating from Breggy and his crew in some back alleyway.

"Let's begin right away, then." Director Quinn said, rising. "I've set up a desk for you by the windows, Miss Smythe, plus a workstation where Lord Atkinson may sit and take notes. In addition, you'll have a direct comm line to the control center. They've been instructed to act immediately upon any information you give them. We don't want any more close-calls like the incident yesterday."

He came around to pull her chair out for her, just as Diana pushed herself away from the table. The director stumbled back, and Lord Atkinson let out a sniff of disapproval.

"Thank you," Diana said, standing awkwardly.

"Yes, yes." Director Quinn waved his hand at her. "You'll pick it up, soon enough."

He opened the door, then paused with an expectant look, and Diana belatedly realized she was supposed to go first. Well, her mishaps would make a good story for her and Tipper to laugh over later, shaking their heads at the silly rules of the gentry.

Her new desk was easy to find. It stood almost exactly in the same spot where she and Director Quinn had watched the ships the day before. It was not as large as the director's gleaming slab of wood, but big enough. A shiny metal box sat on one corner, decorated with knobs and switches. A metal cord snaked out from one side, with some kind of screen-covered nozzle at the end.

Lord Atkinson's work station was set a half meter away, slightly back from the large expanse of the windows, but close enough that he could also observe the ships as they rose and landed.

Just like yesterday, the view made her heart clench with the sheer beauty of it all. While the spaceport itself held a pleasing symmetry, it was the dance of the ships in and out, the trajectories and possibilities, the lives humming and spinning inside, that stole her breath away.

"Will this do?" the director asked.

She nodded, hardly able to take her gaze from the window. "It's splendid."

Despite her own missteps and fears, despite the brooding presence of Lord Atkinson at her shoulder, her life was as near enough to perfect as made no difference.

Director Quinn patted the metal contraption on her desk. "This is your connection to the control center. When you need to speak to them, press the button, here, and use the microphone, like so." He demonstrated, holding the nozzle up to the mouth. "Hello?"

A tinny voice emitted from a grill on the front of the box. "Control speaking."

"This is Director Quinn, on Miss Smythe's direct line. Make a note of it."

"Very good, sir. As requested, we're at the ready here."

"Excellent. Goodbye." The director released the button and set the microphone back in its holder. "You see. It's a clever device, but quite simple to use."

"Yes," Diana said. "I think I can manage."

Had there been a series of speaking tubes installed in the mansion of her childhood? She thought so, but couldn't quite recall. The concept seemed quite familiar, even though the device on her desk was strange to her eye.

"Feel free to call upon me for assistance," Lord Atkinson said, his tone implying that she would need his help.

Diana ignored him, pretending to be engrossed in pulling open the desk drawers to discover their contents.

"I'll leave you to get settled," the director said. "If you need anything, don't hesitate to ask me. Although, as Lord Atkinson said, his help is at the ready.

Diana bobbed another curtsey and let her bland smile include Lord Atkinson. "Thank you."

The director strode away, but Lord Atkinson continued to hover, his arms folded.

"Don't get too cocky," he said in a low voice. "You might be the director's pet at the moment, but that could change."

"I'm here to work. Same as you."

That made him scowl faintly, as it was meant to. Diana

pointedly turned her back on him and settled into her chair. It was one of the comfortable leather-upholstered ones from the conference room, though the seat was a bit too high.

She felt about the edges for a lever to adjust it, then blinked in surprise as Lord Atkinson went down on one knee beside her. He smelled of expensive cologne and freshly laundered linen, and his blue eyes were nearly at a level with hers.

"My apologies," he said. "I'm… that is, this is difficult for me. Please try to understand."

He sounded disarmingly sincere, and Diana blinked at him for a moment, trying to understand his point of view. Surely it couldn't be easy, being suddenly forced to collaborate with some unknown girl fished off the streets. If he wasn't a nob, it might be less of a problem for him, but he was gentry, and she was… well, a grubby streetrat.

And a mathematical genius, she reminded herself. She had every right to be there, and Director Quinn valued what she could do. Besides, if she did not stand up to Lord Atkinson now, she feared he'd always treat her with that edge of contempt.

"All right," she said. "I forgive you. But you'll have to stop being so ill-mannered."

"Ill-mannered?" His nostrils flared. Then he shook his head, the spark of temper in his eyes fading. "I suppose I have been, a little. I'll do my best to change."

She wasn't entirely sure she believed him, but perhaps he was telling the truth. She could at least give him the benefit of the doubt.

"Well then, Lord Atkinson, do we have a truce?"

She stuck out her hand. He gazed at it in surprise, then took it in a firm handshake. His palm was warm against hers, smooth and uncalloused, and she realized she'd made another error in judgment. Ladies didn't shake gentlemen's hands, apparently.

"Please, call me Christopher," he said. "No need to be formal, since we'll be working together."

"I'm Diana," she said. "Now, could you show me how to adjust this dratted chair?"

"The knob, here." He guided her fingers to it, underneath the seat, then stood.

His expression was still a bit haughty, but softer about the mouth and eyes. For the first time since meeting Lord Atkinson, Diana thought that, perhaps, they'd be able to get along, after all.

CHAPTER 14

DIANA STEPPED THROUGH THE DOOR OF NUMBER 54, THEN paused at the delicious smells wafting through the flat. Baking bread, herbs, and was that the smoky sizzle of grilled meat? Her mouth watered at the thought.

In addition to shopping for new clothing that morning, she and Tipper had gone to the market and bought a variety of foodstuffs—at his insistence. She'd indulged him, figuring they'd eat takeaway most nights. But the smells that greeted her suggested otherwise.

"Tip?" she called, hanging up her hat and depositing her reticule by the door.

"Kitchen," he replied.

The sight of Tipper wearing an apron down to his shins made her smile. He stood before the stove, a fork in one hand, prodding a pan full of sausages.

"I… didn't know you could cook," she said.

He grinned at her. "Full of surprises, I am."

"I can't help much in the kitchen, but I'll set the table," she said, suiting action to words.

Before long they were sitting at the small table in the eating nook, tucking in to a lavish spread of sausages, fresh baked biscuits with jam and butter, and a bowl of sliced melons with flesh the color of jade.

As they ate, Diana told Tipper about her afternoon.

"Lord Atkinson sounds like a right stick," Tipper said. "I don't like him."

"I think he means well. And I don't have the luxury of disliking him. After all, we'll be working together."

"Well, watch yourself." Tipper helped himself to the last sausage on the plate. "Nobs are always trouble for our kind."

Diana sighed and wiped her mouth with a cloth napkin. It seemed a waste of good cloth, but she hoped to teach Tipper some manners, leading by example.

"I'm not sure what, exactly, I am anymore," she said, with a twinge of discomfort.

At least as a streetrat, she knew her place in the world. This new life, though… She shook her head.

"You're Di," Tipper said matter-of-factly. "Nothin' changes that."

She fingered the silver chain about her neck. "I was born into the gentry, you know."

"Aye—the moment we first met I knew it." He squinted at her. "You don't hide yer fancy words and airs very well, leastwise not around me."

"I trust you," she said simply. "But how did you learn to cook?"

"My ma was Cook for a big house," he said, expression growing solemn. "She taught me all this when I was just a wee boy." He waved at the table.

He wasn't much bigger now, but Diana bit her lip. Like her, he was small for his age. Spending one's prime growing years rummaging about in rubbish heaps for scraps of food would do that to a body. She'd survived for too long on stolen bits of cheese and the stale ends of loaves, vegetables nearly gone to slime, discarded packets of chips with a few rancid crumbs in the corners…

She took a bite of melon, crisp and sweet, to banish the memories.

"So, you'll be taking up cooking duties for us?" she asked.

"Not breakfast." He sent her a pleading look. "I aim to sleep 'til noon every day."

"I can manage a pot of tea and toast," she assured him. "But what about the rest of your day?"

"I'll find summat to do." His cheery grin was back, and firmly in place.

"Make sure it's on the up and up." She gave him a stern look. "I'll leave money for the grocers."

In truth, though, she *did* trust Tipper. Especially now that he'd demonstrated his cookery skills. Those would help keep him out of trouble, at least for a time.

THE REST OF THE WEEK PASSED UNEVENTFULLY. EVERY morning she rose and fixed herself a simple breakfast, donned one of her new dresses, and took the train down to the spaceport.

Lord Atkinson observed her as she watched the ships,

asking questions that she could not always answer, which left him prickly and frustrated.

It wasn't her fault that she couldn't explain precisely to him how her mind worked, and his irritation with her sparked her animosity in return. She tried to remain reasonable, however, doing her best to narrate her thought processes. It wasn't easy, but she tried to describe how the arcs of parabolas inscribed themselves on the sky, how the possibilities inherent in every movement narrowed down to a single course.

On the other hand, when he wasn't annoyed, he could be quite charming. Slowly he began to treat her less like a piece of trash blown in off the street and more like someone worthy of his grudging respect. He was also a spacecraft enthusiast, well versed in the particulars of each ship and able to identify the more obscure models she wasn't familiar with.

She was relieved to find that common ground. It helped offset the times he'd rise and pace furiously, spending his temper with his feet when she could not tell him what he wanted to know.

Her afternoons were easier without Lord Atkinson's intense focus and insistent questions. She could lose herself in the ebb and flow of the spaceport, graphing equations on her handheld and immersing herself in the pure joy of numbers.

On Friday evening, Nails came by the flat to check on them, as promised. Tipper wheedled her into staying for dinner—a magnificent pot roast with potatoes and carrots, and strawberry pie for dessert. Diana hadn't asked him how much the berries had cost. She suspected the amount would make her wince, and besides, she reminded herself, she could afford it.

On the weekend, she and Tipper walked to the nearby square and enjoyed a lazy picnic.

"Wonder what they're doing in West Quay," he said, laying back to watch the clouds skim across the sky. "Bet Breggy's steamed we've gone missing."

"I don't want to think about it," Diana said, packing the remains of their lunch back into the wicker basket.

Her life as a streetrat was done, and Breggy's reach didn't extend up Queensway. She hoped.

On her commute in and out of the spaceport, she was careful not to look at the beggars on their various corners. She didn't think she'd be recognized, but one never knew. Streetrats were clever and observant, and the last thing she needed was to draw attention to her new status.

Though what Breggy could do about it, she didn't know.

"I've a mind to look for work," Tipper said, rolling over and plucking a piece of grass to chew on.

"Oh? You've no references."

"Nails said she'd put in a word for me at the pub down the street. They need a dish boy, but I can work my way up in the kitchen, 'fore long."

"No doubt you can." She ruffled his somewhat greasy hair. "Take a bath before you apply, right?"

He let out an exaggerated sigh, then smiled up at her. Already the hollows of his cheeks were filling in, the cuts now healed from where Breggy had backhanded him. Of course, not all the injuries they carried from the streets were visible, or would mend cleanly.

But for the moment, she would take what peace she could.

CHAPTER 15

DEREK RUBBED THE BACK OF HIS NECK, FEELING THE SWEAT and grime of the summer day collect against his fingers. He stared down again at the handwritten note on his desk, delivered by a discreet courier from the other side of the river. It read:

The inscription on the ring translates loosely into the galactic smuggler's motto, secretum est optimus. *Hidden treasure is best. Good luck.*

Wonderful. The corpse they'd pulled from the river two months ago was involved with the spacegoing smugglers. Was this similar to the deadly jostling for position among the gangrunners, or was something more sinister afoot?

He shook his head, trying to focus. It was difficult to think past the undercurrent of worry he'd carried for the last fortnight. Diana and Tipper had disappeared. Gone, like rainwater evaporating after a storm, and he had no clue how to find them.

Every time a report of a body came, he steeled himself

for what he'd find. So far, his worst fears hadn't come true, but he suspected it was only a matter of time.

He hadn't been able to save his brother, who'd died in a deadly bombing in the pursuit of Ireland's freedom. Maybe Derek was trying to make amends for that by protecting those two streetrats—balancing the scales, as it were. In truth, the world would be an emptier place without Diana, with her quick mind and clear-eyed gaze, and young Tipper, clever and scrappy.

Damnú, why hadn't they taken his offer of tickets up to London? Was Derek destined to lose every person he allowed himself to care for, even the tiniest bit?

He picked up the message from the Turkish bath owner and crumpled it in his fist. His contacts in the Irish Nationalist Resistance were unhappy that he hadn't yet been able to provide them current intelligence from inside the spaceport. The fate of two streetrats shouldn't get in the way of that mission.

This lead was the perfect opportunity to gain access to Spaceport Security, maybe even the inner sanctum of the director's office. And he'd take it, truly he would, but first he had a raid to organize.

If Diana and Tipper weren't dead—which hope he stubbornly clung to, since their bodies hadn't surfaced—there was only one place they could be.

Breggy's.

Diana had given him the location of the gangrunner's hideout, and he hadn't acted on the information. Yet. But he was sure he could convince Headquarters to approve the raid and send reinforcements. Cribbs would back him up. The other officer was always in favor of a violent show of strength.

As soon as his shift was over, Derek would make a visit to his superior officer at the Greater Southampton Police Headquarters. Within a day or two, the plan would be in place. They had to move quickly, so that none of Breggy's crew caught wind of it.

There was always the risk that Diana and Tipper might be hurt during the raid, or taken into custody before Derek could intervene, but he had to do *something*.

He ran his fingers through his hair. One thing at a time. First, extricate Diana and Tipper from Breggy's clutches. Once they were safe, he'd make an appointment with Spaceport Security to discuss the body the police had fished out of the Itchen.

"Where are they?" Derek leaned in to the handcuffed gangrunner, anger spiking through his veins, and took a fistful of Breggy's shirt, close to the neck.

If he had to choke the information out of the man, he'd do it, and no regrets.

Breggy's face was fitfully illuminated by the last remnants of the fire the police had set to smoke the gang out of their hiding place. He smiled—more a grimace—his gold tooth shining.

"Don't know who you mean."

Derek's grip tightened. "Di—Diver, and Tipper."

"Those two." Breggy spat out a clot of blood. "Gone."

He hadn't been taken without a fight, and Derek could feel the bruises rising on his own ribs and across his jaw. During the raid, the force had rounded up most of the Breggy's deputies. They couldn't arrest the entire crew, however, and a number of the streetrats had been let go—those not deemed to be a threat, those too young for full transportation.

None of them had been Diana or Tipper.

"Gone where?" Derek asked.

If Breggy said the bottom of the river, Derek feared he'd be hard put not to end the man then and there. Simple enough to tell Headquarters he'd died in the fight.

"Wherever traitors go." Breggy gave him a sly look. "Thought you'd taken them in, copper. Seeing as how you've a fancy for young boys."

Diana's secret was still safe, then. Derek blew a breath out his nostrils and refrained from punching the gangrunner right in the center of that bright golden smirk.

"They did me in, didn't they?" Breggy continued, his expression hardening. "Streetrats turning on their own. If I ever catch up to them, they'll wish they were dead."

"That won't happen, as you're bound for transportation, and your bullyboys with you." Derek hoped it was to one of the harder worlds, too, where convicts didn't last more than a few years.

"Aye? I'm warning you, I always settle my debts, copper. And I've got friends in high places." Breggy's voice was deadly serious.

"You won't be talking so bold when you're bound for a prison planet," Derek said. Despite his words, cold premonition prickled the back of his neck.

One of the officers from Headquarters came up to Derek. "Done here, Officer Byrne?"

"Aye. Take him away." Derek let go of Breggy's shirt, relief warring with worry.

If Diana and Tipper weren't here, and weren't dead, then where, in the name of all the stars, could they be?

CHAPTER 16

"Miss Smythe," Lord Atkinson said, at the beginning of their fourth week of working together, "might I have the pleasure of escorting you to a ball?"

Diana swiveled her chair about and blinked at him. Was this some kind of trap? Well, she didn't intend to fall into it.

"I'm not gentry," she said.

"I'm well aware of the fact." His lip curled, ever so slightly. "Still, the monthly People's Cotillion will be held this coming Thursday, at the Royal Victoria Assembly rooms. It's not just for the nobility, so you may set your mind at ease."

"Why ask me?"

He glanced to one side, the faintest flush visible on his neck. "Is it a crime to want to purse a young lady's company outside of business hours? I find you interesting, Diana."

Her thoughts stuttered about in her head. Surely Lord

Atkinson wasn't implying a romantic interest in her? It was most unexpected—and unlikely.

"I don't dance." At least, she didn't *think* she knew how.

"It's not difficult." His gaze returned to her face. "You've demonstrated an impressive grasp of numbers. Dancing is simply counting to the beat, and moving your feet accordingly."

"I'm certain it's a bit more involved than that."

"Well, perhaps so." He gave her a half smile. "But I'm considered an excellent dancing partner, not to be too modest. I'll take care of you."

She didn't particularly *want* to be taken care of, and certainly not by a somewhat irritating member of the nobility. And yet, the idea of attending a ball held a certain appeal. It reminded her of a tale her Nanny had once told her, about a princess and a glass slipper…

The memory slipped away, but not the feeling of possibility.

"Very well," she said. "I'll go to the ball with you."

"You will?" Now it was his turn to blink in surprise. Then his smile widened with satisfaction. "I didn't think you'd say yes. At least, not the first time I asked."

Should she have put him off? Ah well, too late now.

The firing of a Frauke's engines in a nearby berth made them both turn back to the window, and their work. But still, she was going to a ball! The thought shimmered through Diana, half pleasure, half panic.

What in the heavens was she going to wear?

Lord Atkinson promised to fetch her from Queensway Tower promptly at eight o'clock on Thursday evening. At quarter-til-eight, Diana was waiting in the foyer, feeling absurdly overdressed. Her nano-lifted skirts of deep blue had almost gotten caught in the lift doors, and she cursed the impulse that had made her purchase the extravagant ball gown. No matter how much the gauzy drift put her mind of cloud nebulas, the gown was ridiculously impractical.

Much more sensible to wear something that cooperated with the laws of gravity—but it was too late now. Besides, she didn't think one of her high-collared work dresses would go over well with Lord Atkinson. One wore ball gowns to balls, after all.

And, according to the modiste, elbow-length gloves, dancing slippers with discreet heels, and as much jewelry as Diana could manage.

Which wasn't much, admittedly. Her large salary was quickly disappearing in the face of the expenses of her new life. Still, she'd had enough to purchase an elegant sapphire necklace and matching earrings.

You can always sell them off later, she reminded herself.

"Coo, don't you look fine," Tipper had said when she'd emerged from her bedroom. "All the toffest nobs'll want to dance with you."

She'd grimaced. "Provided I don't trip over my own feet."

"A nice bit of flash, too." He'd nodded at her jewelry.

"Foolishness." She'd set her hand to the jewels about her neck. "We could've lived off this for nigh on a year, on the streets."

"Aye, but we'd still be sleeping in the rubble, and trying to stay away from Breggy. I like this much better."

"So do I."

Every day, her fear that it would be all snatched away faded a bit more. Although—and she knew it was beyond foolish—a strange discontent had begun to take its place. It was all very well helping Lord Atkinson with his device and smoothing out the daily routine of the spaceport, but it was not the future she had envisioned for herself.

Aye, she was helping others reach the stars, but every time a ship blasted off, a tiny bit of her heart went with it. She wanted to go *into* the blue, not just watch from the outside.

She was saving up, of course, for passage out, but that still did not feel like an answer. Not a complete one.

And now here she was, pacing in the foyer, catching glimpses of herself in the gilt-framed mirror beside the lift. Tipper had helped her put her hair up, and she'd let the jeweler talk her into a sparkling headpiece. From the outside, she looked the very picture of a lady of Quality.

Except for a few ever-present banknotes tucked in her corset, and a collarbone that still jutted out a bit too sharply for the well-fed beauty of the gentry. The gloves hadn't wanted to stay up, either, until the modiste had given her a small bottle of glue.

"All the ladies use it," she'd said. "It will hold your gown precisely upon your shoulders, without slipping scandalously down. And it will serve to keep your gloves secure, too. Our little secret."

Diana hoped she'd be able to remove her gloves and gown when the evening was over. How long did it take for the glue to wear off? What if it lost its stickiness too soon? More anxieties, piled upon her cartload of worries. Oh, why had she told Lord Atkinson yes?

Just as she was considering retreating back to the safety of Number 54, a gorgeously gilded carriage arrived drawn by two matching gray horses. The footman riding on the back of the vehicle hopped down and opened the door, and Lord Atkinson stepped out into the evening air.

Diana was accustomed to his elegant mode of dress at the spaceport, but this was exponentially more refined. He wore a perfectly tailored black suit with long tails, and a blue waistcoat that, she was glad to see, nearly matched the color of her gown. She'd gambled that he'd, as usual, wear something that matched his eyes, and she'd been right. A large diamond stickpin glittered in his crisp white neck cloth, and his hair was artfully disheveled.

Thank all the stars she'd purchased the ridiculous gown after all, otherwise she would have looked quite the drab little crow beside Lord Atkinson's magnificence.

Clutching her reticule, blue satin, to match her underskirts, Diana went to open the front door.

"My dear Diana!" Lord Atkinson caught the door and held it wide for her. His gaze raked her from head to toe and for a moment she thought she saw a spark of irritation in his eyes.

But that was ridiculous. Surely it was admiration.

"How beautiful you look." He sounded quite sincere as held out his arm to escort her to the coach. "I'll be the envy of every man there."

"Thank you, my lord."

"Christopher," he said, handing her into the carriage. "I insist."

It felt too personal, but he *did* keep calling her Diana. Perhaps it was his attempt to set her at ease instead of emphasizing the class differences between them.

The interior of the carriage was lit with a softly glowing lightstrip mounted overhead. The ornate gilding on the outside of the vehicle carried along over the ceiling; golden vines curling in loops and whorls that made her a bit dizzy to trace.

Lord Atkinson—she simply could not think of him as Christopher—settled on the bench seat across from her.

"Would you like the curtains closed, or do you prefer to enjoy the view?" he asked

"Open please," she said. "How far are we going?"

It was always a good idea to know where she was headed, and how to get back again. Just in case.

He turned a knob that dimmed the lights, then pulled back the thick velvet curtains as the carriage pulled away from Queensway Tower.

"The assembly rooms are on Portland Terrace," he said. "We'll be there soon."

She nodded as if the information meant anything to her, and looked out the window. The carriage was going past the green swath of Houndwell Park. The sun was not quite down, but the gas lamps had been lit. A row of them led off between the trees, and for a moment Diana wanted to jump out of the vehicle and follow them to some quiet, green, magical place.

Instead, she convoluted the Fibonacci sequence in her head, letting the flow of numbers calm her nerves. The precise equations were much more relaxing than the tangle of golden vines decorating the carriage ceiling overhead.

Lord Atkinson seemed content to leave her to her silence, and several minutes passed before the carriage slowed and came to a stop.

"Here we are," he said, leaning forward. "Don't be nervous, Diana."

"I'm not." It was mostly true.

She let go of her calculations and looked out the window. They had come to a halt beside a long two-story building surrounded by lush gardens. Balconies ran around the upper floor, and light streamed from the high windows set at regular intervals along the sides.

As Lord Atkinson handed her out of the coach, she heard music drifting from above—violins, flutes, the lower tones of a cello. Groups of people clustered on the lawn, some smoking cheroots, others engaged in a game of rolling balls on the close-clipped grass.

The balls, some larger, some smaller, glowed in the twilight. She faintly remembered playing such a game— and that her older siblings had banned her from it, since she always won.

Lord Atkinson escorted her to the portico covered entryway. As they stepped inside she was relieved to see that, indeed, there were a variety of people in attendance, seemingly of several different classes. While there were a fair number of lords and ladies in evidence, she also spotted a group of quiet young ladies in subdued gowns, gentlemen in serviceable suits, and a bunch of matrons knitting in the far corner.

"Shall we?" Lord Atkinson gestured to the grand staircase ascending to the ballroom.

"Yes." She hoped she could manage her skirts without making a fool of herself.

When they got to the top, she let out a breath. She ought to have trusted the nano-lifter's technology, for the gauzy overskirt had floated perfectly about her with each step. The true test, of course, would be when she danced.

They went along the landing, the patterned carpet giving way to polished oak as they arrived at one end of the long room. Inside was a flurry of light and motion, heat and perfume. Diana's pulse rose, and despite herself she couldn't help cataloging the value of the jewelry sparkling at throats and wrists, the shiny lure of gold pocket watches.

The wealth in this room could feed and clothe an entire army of streetrats.

On one side of the room, a raised balcony held the small orchestra safely above the whirl of dancers. On the other, the tall windows were open, letting in a much-needed breeze that fluttered the dark curtains. Double-tiered chandeliers hung from the ceiling, crystals sparkling in the gaslight.

Lord Atkinson led her forward, past the clots of people talking around the edges, until they had a clear view of the floor.

"When they announce the next dance, we'll find a place," he said.

"What if I don't know the steps?"

He gave her a superior smile, and she wondered again if he'd brought her here to humiliate her, after all.

"Really, Diana, you must trust me."

I don't. She didn't voice the thought aloud.

"Remind me again—why did you invite me to come dancing?" she asked.

He pressed her gloved hand. "As I said, for the pleasure of your company. And, frankly, to see what you would do. You are a curious young woman."

"Wait." She pulled her hand from his and took a step away. "Do you mean this to be some kind of experiment? I'm not your prize, to be fished off the streets and turned into your idea of a proper lady, you know."

He looked at her, expression serious. "I must say, you don't seem to need my help in that arena. You certainly exceeded my expectations with your gown."

"I'm not an utter fool."

"I never thought so. Please, Diana." He extended his hand. "I know I can be an insufferable fellow at times. Give me another chance."

She didn't have to, of course. She could demand he return her to Queensway Tower, or, if he refused, she could even walk home.

But she was at a ball, and dressed for it, whether her escort liked it or not. She might as well stay for at least one dance.

"Very well." Diana placed her hand back in Lord Atkinson's.

"Thank you," he said, giving her a smile tinged with apology.

The look of relief on his face mollified her somewhat. Perhaps he was simply nervous. It was true she probably behaved quite differently than the highborn young women he was accustomed to.

The music came to a close. Amid the light smattering of applause, one of the violinists on the balcony stood. "The next dance will be the polka mazurka," she announced in a loud voice before resuming her seat.

"Ah." Lord Atkinson glanced down at Diana. "This is a somewhat strenuous step. If you don't feel ready yet, I understand. We can wait until the orchestra plays something simple."

"What is the timing for a mazurka?" she asked.

For some reason, she wanted to prove she could do this; likely because of the doubtful look in his eye.

"Three, but it's quicker than most waltzes."

"Let's watch a moment, and then I'll be ready." She hoped.

As it turned out, the mazurka was an active dance, but not particularly difficult. She spotted the pattern right away: step-step-hop to the right, repeated, then switching to the left for two more repetitions of the step, and so on.

"It looks simple enough," she said.

Lord Atkinson opened his arms, and there was an awkward moment as she tried to figure out where to put her hands. A quick glance at the next couple over showed her the placement. Right hand clasped in his, left hand resting on his shoulder.

He cinched her in a bit closer, his arm firmly about her waist. It was a rather unsettling sensation, to be so close to him, and she wasn't sure if she liked it or not.

"On my count," he said softly. "One. Two. Three."

Then they were off, and she ceased being aware of his nearness. All her concentration was caught up in moving her feet quickly enough to stay with the music. The dance hadn't looked quite so fast from the sidelines.

She accidentally kicked Lord Atkinson in the ankles a few times as they hopped about the dance floor. Luckily she was wearing soft-toed dancing slippers and not her sturdy boots. Just when she was afraid she'd start gasping for breath, the music slowed, then came to a halt.

Lord Atkinson released her and swept her a bow. A heartbeat later she made him a belated curtsy, her skirts bobbing like stardust.

"You picked that up quite well," he said, his face slightly flushed from the exertion of the dance.

"It was rather fun," she said. "Especially as we didn't careen into anyone else."

"I would never let that happen," he said, sounding haughty again. "Are you ready for a glass of punch? The refreshment rooms are below."

"Certainly."

He held out his arm, and she set her gloved hand upon it. Astounding to think she was here, begowned and bejeweled, dancing with a member of the nobility, when less than a month ago she'd been sleeping in the streets.

CHAPTER 17

Derek stood in the garden outside the Royal Victoria Assembly Rooms, sweating slightly in his suit. It was a heavy, old-fashioned thing that had belonged to his father. When he'd left for England, his ma had insisted he pack it along.

"Never know when ye'll be needing a suit, now," she'd said, folding it into the half-full trunk with the rest of his clothing.

As it turned out, she was right, though he didn't think she'd approve of Derek wearing it to clandestine meetings with a representative of the Irish Nationalist Resistance. Still, the monthly People's Cotillion was a safe enough place to make contact—especially as said contact was a lovely redhead named Molly O'Rourke.

It was the perfect cover. When they sat, heads close together, everyone would assume they were courting, not exchanging critical information about the spaceport's protocols. Besides, no one he knew would ever frequent the ball.

This was the third time he'd been directed to meet with Molly and update her on his progress, though she hadn't yet arrived. Or perhaps she had, and was waiting for him inside. Their communications were nearly non-existent, the danger of discovery too high.

Neither of them could afford to jeopardize his mission of infiltrating the spaceport. Any hint of a connection between Officer Byrne and the radical freedom movement of the INR would dash that plan altogether.

It wasn't Derek's choice, truth be told. But it had been Seamus's, and he'd died for it. *Because of me.*

His soul was weighted with the unpaid debt. Grim memories rose of that day everything had changed—the day he'd discovered that his brother was involved in a planned bombing of the Irish Parliament. He'd raced to Dublin's city center and burst in on the scene.

It was the bitterest of ironies, that his arrival had triggered the INR to act too soon.

Derek still recalled that horrified second when he'd seen Seamus's face—so young, so determined—before the blast had shattered the building. And Derek's heart.

Not long after, the resistance had come calling.

He shook his shoulders, trying to dispel the memories that still clung to him like the dust after the explosion. Seamus was gone, but the INR remained.

And Molly was late. Derek consulted his dented steel pocket watch. Ten minutes past their appointed meeting time. He'd best go inside and see if he might "accidentally" encounter his contact among the dancers.

He scanned the crowd as he ascended the wide, carpeted steps, but there was no sign of his contact. Finally he glimpsed her at the far edge of the dance floor, chatting with a tall blond woman. He caught Molly's eye, and she gave him a barely perceptible nod.

It was harder than it looked to make his way through the crowd. A dance had just finished, and he was swimming upstream against the exodus of couples on their way off the floor. He was nearly to Molly, when his way was blocked by a young lady wearing extravagantly nano-lifted skirts.

"Begging your pardon," he said, beginning to sidle about the woman.

"Officer Byrne?"

The familiar voice brought him up short, and his startled gaze went to the lady's face.

"Diana?" He couldn't believe it.

She must have a twin in the gentry somehow, for surely the streetrat known as Diver couldn't be here, so elegantly dressed and on the arm of an equally stylish gentleman.

"Yes, it's me." She gave him a tentative smile.

They stood there a moment, gazing at one another. Derek felt quite dumbfounded to see her, jewels at her throat, wearing gloves, her hair upswept and fastened with a glittering headpiece. For her part, she seemed equally at a loss for words.

What happened? Where have you been? I was worried about you. Why are you dressed so grandly? Where's Tipper? The questions crowded his brain, and he couldn't sort out which to ask first.

The lord escorting her cleared his throat.

"Might I ask who this fellow is?" He looked at Diana, his expression disapproving.

"Oh, yes." Seeming a bit flustered, she glanced between them. "Er, Lord Atkinson, this is Office Byrne, of the Southampton police."

"Pleased to meet you." Derek stuck out his hand. Despite the confusion rocketing through him, it was always best to be polite with the gentry.

After a moment, Lord Atkinson took his hand and gave it a quick, brisk shake. His lip curled up the slightest bit as he looked from Derek to Diana.

"I take it you two have a prior acquaintance?"

Before Derek could form an answer that wouldn't embarrass her, Diana nodded.

"I met Officer Byrne when I was on the streets," she said. "And I'm not too proud to admit it. He helped me out a time or two."

"Oh?" The nobleman's eyebrows rose. "*Kind* to you, was he?"

The words were heavy with double meaning, and a flash of temper went through Derek. His lordship's insinuations were not only incorrect, it was beyond rude to imply that Diana was nothing but a common doxy.

"Is common decency to those less fortunate something you're unfamiliar with, my lord?" Derek asked.

Diana's lips twitched, as though she were trying to hide a smile, while her escort's nostrils flared.

"You're not the only one to notice that Miss Smythe is a remarkable young lady," Lord Atkinson said. "Though I would never take advantage of her past."

"Nor would I."

The animosity coming off the man made Derek square his shoulders and wish for his stunclub. Lord Atkinson seemed to have a proprietary yet dismissive attitude about Diana, and Derek did not much care for it. He shifted his gaze to her.

"Would you care to dance?"

"I would." She darted a glance at her escort. "That is, if Lord Atkinson doesn't mind."

The nobleman sniffed. "Far be it from me to dictate who you associate with. If you'd like to dance with Officer Byrne, then by all means do so."

She either didn't hear or chose to ignore the sarcasm in his words. Giving him a bright smile, she let go of his arm.

"Then I shall. Thank you." She turned to Derek, who hastily offered his hand.

"Be advised," Lord Atkinson said to him, "Diana is not a particularly experienced dancer. My skills enabled us to navigate the floor without issue, but you might encounter some difficulty in that regard."

Derek swallowed back the hot retort at the tip of his tongue. It would do none of them any good to let his Irish temper free. Bad enough that he'd been seen at the ball, but even worse if he were to draw undue attention by socking the pompous Lord Atkinson in the jaw.

"Noted," he said shortly.

Then, before Lord Atkinson could say anything more, Derek set his hand to Diana's satin-clad back and whisked her away through the thinning crowd.

"Tell me everything," he said, guiding her to a quiet alcove. He hoped he didn't sound too much like an officer interrogating a prisoner. "Is Tipper all right? Are you? What's your connection to that Lord Atkinson fellow?"

"It's not what you might think," she said, flushing

slightly. "I'm not… associating with Lord Atkinson in return for…that is, I'm not his mistress."

He blinked at her. "The thought didn't cross my mind," he said.

It was true. And rather ironic that Diana's escort had immediately assumed the worst of her and Derek, while Derek had seen her richly dressed on his lordship's arm and hadn't for a moment considered that she'd traded her favors to be there.

"Well then." She gazed at him from her clear gray eyes. "Do you know how to dance?"

"Not very well," he admitted. "But depending on what they call next, I might be able to manage."

Her look turned considering. "If you're not a very good dancer, then why did you come to the ball?" she asked.

"It seemed something to do," he lied, then distracted her with more questions. "But why are you here? And what about Tipper?"

She smiled. "Tip's well, and turning into quite the cook. As for myself, I've a job at the spaceport now. It's where I met Lord Atkinson."

"You're working at the spaceport?" He couldn't help the incredulity in his voice. It was the last thing he'd imagined when she'd disappeared from the streets.

Her smile faded. "Whatever you might think, Officer Byrne, I don't believe one's past controls one's future."

Her words hit him in the gut.

"Of course it does," he said reflexively. Only look at his own life.

She tipped her head. "If you think so, then you make your own truth. But a tiny course adjustment, applied at the right time, can result in a very different outcome. Any mathematician knows as much."

"I don't pretend to be one," he said, feeling suddenly out of his depth. "I only meant, I was worried about you. I'd feared the worst."

"Oh." Comprehension dawned in her eyes. "I'm sorry—I should have sent word. I didn't think you'd fret over us."

"I did." He didn't feel the need to mention he'd lost sleep over her for the better part of a month. "In fact, I organized a raid on Breggy's, thinking he'd got the two of you into his clutches."

Her eyes widened. "I never thought you cared."

"I did care." He caught her hand. "I still do."

Their gazes caught. Held.

"If ever I leave again, I'll tell you before I go," she said in a soft voice. "I promise."

"Thank you." His heart thumped in his chest, so loudly it drowned out every other thought.

A burst of laughter sounded by a nearby group of gentlemen and Diana blinked, as if recalling they stood in the midst of a crowded ballroom. That single, trembling moment was gone.

"At any rate," she said, her voice turning brisk, "you must come over for dinner sometime. I'm sure Tipper would be delighted to astound you with his cookery skills."

Derek wanted to accept immediately. But despite the growing sense of connection between them, he was still Officer Byrne.

"I don't imagine Tipper would be too happy to host the man who arrested him," he said.

On the other hand—and he felt like a worm for even

thinking it—Diana had daily access to the spaceport, and could help provide the information about the shipping routes the INR needed. The resistance hadn't elaborated on their plans, but Derek gathered that they planned to smuggle political fugitives off-planet, out of reach of the Empire's cruel justice.

"Ahem." A woman's voice cut into their conversation. "Sorry to interrupt."

He glanced up to see Molly O'Rourke standing before them, hands on her hips and a look of annoyance on her face.

"Miss O'Rourke," he said, feeling suddenly guilty. "I was hoping to cross paths with you this evening."

Despite the awkwardness of the situation, it was probably best if he and Molly kept up the appearance of courtship.

"Were you, now?" She sent a pointed look at his hand, clasped with Diana's.

"Yes." He let go. "I'm afraid I've promised this next dance to Miss Smythe, but I beg you to save the following dance for me."

He kept his gaze on Molly's face, aware that Diana was watching them both.

"If you insist." Molly lifted her nose. "Really, Officer Byrne, I didn't think you were the kind to play lightly with a lady's heart."

"I'm not." *Damnú*, how had he gotten into this mess? And how was he going to get out? "You know you're the one for me, Molly."

"And don't you forget it!" She shot Diana a haughty look, then turned and walked away, her back very straight.

Derek hoped she wasn't laughing at him.

"My apologies." He turned back to Diana. "I did come here to meet Molly. I should've told you so."

"You don't owe me any explanations, officer." She sounded a trifle unhappy, which pleased him an unreasonable amount. "I should bid you a good evening, I suppose."

"But what about our dance? You *did* promise, and I'd like to dance with you."

She flushed slightly. "If you insist. I believe they are announcing a waltz."

"Excellent news," he said, "as I can count to three."

That earned him a slight smile. "You'll be glad to hear that I can, as well."

"Then we're well matched." He held out his arm to her. "Shall we?"

They found a spot on the dance floor, and he took her in the proper hold. Her gauzy blue skirts drifted around them. Despite their utter impracticality, he had to admit they had a certain appeal—as long as they didn't get in the way of the dancing.

The orchestra struck up the music and he took the first step, only to have Diana go in the opposite direction.

"I'm sorry," he said as they stumbled to a halt.

"No." She looked up at him, eyes shining with amusement. "I believe that was entirely my fault. I'll begin on the right next time. Ready?"

He nodded, and at the next downbeat they tried again. This time they both went the same way, and it didn't take long to adjust his steps to the rhythm of the dance. It was more of a challenge to steer them safely around the other couples on the dance floor, and for a few moments his concentration was fully taken up with that task.

Then they reached a clearer portion of the floor and he risked a glance down at her face. It was still difficult to believe that the streetrat known as Diver was now this elegantly-dressed young woman waltzing with him at a ball, sapphires sparkling about her neck, her dark blonde hair held up by an ornate headpiece.

And yet, she did not look out of place.

Whether dressed as a ragged boy, a young woman visiting the Turkish baths, or a lady of Quality, Miss Diana Smythe had the ability to seem perfectly at home in her surroundings.

"What manner of work are you doing at the spaceport?" he asked.

"Counting the ships." She gave him a slightly mischievous look.

Very well, he'd rise to the bait.

"How many do they have?" he asked, keeping his expression serious.

"That's the real question now, isn't it? They keep coming and going, you see."

"Good thing you're there to keep an eye on them."

"It is." There was a somber note in her voice now. "The truth is, I helped avert a major crash, and the director gave me a job on the spot."

It was an answer that only created more questions in his mind, but he really couldn't subject her to a full interrogation there on the dance floor.

"I take it you and Tipper have a flat somewhere?"

"Number 54, in Queensway Tower. As I said, you should come visit."

"That's rather a step up from West Quay."

"I know." She blinked, once. "It's a bit of getting used to, how things have changed."

"Well, I'm very glad to hear it."

And those jagged nights where he lay awake, counting his dead, would have two fewer names. It was a blessing. As was this moment, holding her in his arms and counting to three, over and over again.

Too soon, the waltz ended. He had a hundred more questions to ask her, but Molly O'Rourke was marching determinedly toward them from the edge of the floor.

"Thank you for the dance," Diana said. "We didn't do too badly, after all."

"It was my pleasure." He bowed over her hand.

She glanced up, seeing Molly approach. "You're welcome to come to dinner. And bring Miss O'Rourke, if you'd like. How about Saturday?"

"I'd like that." Though he had no intention of hauling his INR contact along.

Behind Diana's shoulder, he glimpsed Lord Atkinson striding toward them. Clearly their interlude was at an end.

When she arrived, Molly threaded her arm through his. In turn, Lord Atkinson offered his elbow to Diana, and with cordially insincere nods all around, they parted ways.

Molly steered Derek to the stairwell, and then outside, without saying a word. Finally, when they reached the shelter of a large rosebush, she let go of his arm.

"What was that all about?" she asked, her voice sharp. "I

thought you didn't know any of the gentry. Do you realize the danger you've put us in?"

He raised his palms in protest. "I swear to you, meeting Diana took me by complete surprise. The last time I saw her, she was dressed in tattered trousers, on her way to pick pockets at the Southampton docks."

"Then she's a deep undercover operative?" Molly's expression darkened even more. "Are you sure she's to be trusted?"

"She's not precisely an operative."

"Then who is she affiliated with?"

The whole thing felt too complicated to explain, so he fell back on the easiest answer. "She's working for the director of the spaceport."

"Ah." The storm clouds in Molly's eyes cleared. "I see why you're pursuing her."

"I'm not doing any such thing."

Her brows rose. "Whatever you say. But by all means, plan to have dinner with her."

"It's not like that."

She just kept looking at him, skepticism clear on her face. *Damnú*, women were such difficult creatures.

"It would be beneficial if you could infiltrate the spaceport sooner, rather than later," she said. "The last ship carrying colonists to New Eire is filling up. If we don't act soon, our homeland will be empty."

Maybe it's better that way. He didn't speak the thought aloud. In memory of Seamus, in penance for the deaths he'd helped cause, Derek was bound to the INR. He didn't know if he'd ever finish making amends for the past.

"I'm doing my best," he said.

"Do better." She frowned. "By the end of the month, my superiors will expect to hear you've gained access to the spaceport. Don't disappoint them."

"I won't."

Though, in truth, he didn't think he could stomach using his connection to Diana to pump her for information. Things between them were complicated enough as it was.

Did a streetrat-turned-respectable and a policeman helping a known terrorist organization even have a future together?

He supposed the only way to find out was by trying.

CHAPTER 18

Diana was settled at her desk by the vast spaceport window the next morning, charting the ships as they rose and fell, when Lord Atkinson strode up. He set a small box tied with a silver bow on the corner of her desk.

"Good morning," he said. "I wanted to bring you a little something, as a thank you for attending the ball with me."

It was a peace offering. Reluctantly pulling her attention from the bustle below, Diana looked at the gift. Would she accept it?

After she'd danced with Officer Byrne, Lord Atkinson had been decidedly cool toward her. They'd only danced one more set, and then he'd made a flimsy excuse to whisk her back home.

He'd walked her to the entry of Queensway Tower, bowed over her hand, and scarcely waited for the door to close behind her before he was back in his carriage, driving away.

It had left her feeling off balance and uncertain. She wasn't familiar with the rules of the gentry, but she certainly didn't feel she owed Lord Atkinson anything, simply because she'd attended the ball with him.

Perhaps he thought otherwise, or that she shouldn't have danced with anyone other than him. Or maybe he was jealous of Officer Byrne and the connection they shared.

She let out a low breath. At least on the streets, people's motives were clear, no matter how unsavory.

"Please, take it," Lord Atkinson said. "I fear I behaved rather poorly toward you at the end of the evening last night, and I'd like to apologize."

"Why did you?" She met his gaze, and he was the first to glance away.

"I… didn't like to see you dancing with that other fellow," he said. "I know it's foolish of me."

His words rang true, but she didn't think Lord Atkinson was growing fond of her. Rather, she had the uncomfortable suspicion he regarded her as somehow his property. Would his attitude be different if he knew she'd been born into the nobility?

For the first time in a long while, Diana considered what it would mean to claim her heritage. Provided anyone believed her.

Officer Byrne would. The thought came unbidden.

In truth, she wanted to be accepted for who she was. Streetrat, working woman, well-born young lady; she was still Diana underneath, no matter the label.

Lord Atkinson was still looking at her, a slightly pleading look on his face. Which, for such an insufferable toff, was akin to begging her with hands clasped. She glanced at the box on her desk.

"Very well." She pulled it over and untied the silver ribbon. "I accept your apology."

Mostly in the interests of keeping their working relationship amicable.

She lifted the lid off the box to reveal a delicate clockwork flower set on a crystalline base. The center was intricately geared, the five closed petals surrounding it enameled with rose and gold. Carefully she pulled it out and set it on her desk, next to the communication device.

"Thank you," she said. "It's lovely."

And rather useless. Just the thing a lord would give a gently-bred young lady—a beautiful, useless trinket.

She could buy herself any trinket she wanted, she realized, and for a half-second she contemplated the possibilities. What might she like? A light-pistol, perhaps? Or one of those gadgets that held a dozen different tools, each one tucked ingeniously away in a different part of the handle?

"Give it a moment," Lord Atkinson said, gesturing to the clockwork blossom. "It responds to light... Ah, there we go."

The flower whirred, gears turning, and the petals opened with a graceful mechanical unfurling.

"How clever." She set her hand over the base, guessing that was where the light-sensing mechanism was located.

He intuition proved correct. After a moment the petals slowly closed back up into their original position. Smiling, she removed her hand and watched as the flower opened again. It was amusing, she'd give it that much. And speaking of mechanisms...

"How is your Calculations Device coming along?" she

asked. It seemed that over the last few days he'd been a bit less frustrated, and she was glad of the change.

"Well enough." He leaned against the side of her desk. "Thanks to watching you, I've been able to run several successful simulations, modeling actual trajectories you've observed here."

"That's the aim, isn't it?"

"Indeed." He smiled at her. "Since not every spaceport in the galaxy can have a Diana Smythe working with the control center, my program will be able to replicate much of the work you do here. Why, in another fortnight, you'll be quite replaceable."

"Oh." She wasn't sure how she felt about a device replicating her unique skills—but Lord Atkinson did have a point.

Southampton Spaceport might be the Empire's gateway to the stars, but as colonists spread throughout the galaxy, other hubs were becoming essential. Clearly, the type of work she was doing could benefit other ports, other space stations. Lord Atkinson's Calculations Device could be quite helpful.

Elsewhere.

The lift dinged at the end of the large room, heralding someone's arrival. Diana paid it no mind. People came and went all day, meeting with Director Quinn to discuss the minutiae of running the spaceport.

"What's he doing here?" Lord Atkinson asked, scowling.

"Who?" Diana swiveled her chair, to see the new arrival pause at Le's desk.

Uniformed, dark hair—it was Office Byrne. Her breath caught for a moment. Did this have anything to do with seeing one another at the ball? Was he there to verify she was telling the truth about her employment?

Then he glanced up and smiled at her, and her pulse notched back down. She had nothing to fear from him.

Except her own reaction, which was not practical in the least. Yes, attraction was a force in the universe, but it was too weak to keep two bodies in a steady orbit. Particularly ones with their own, independent, trajectories.

Le spoke with Officer Byrne for a moment and then nodded toward Director Quinn's desk. And though she was inclined—quite foolishly—to jump up and greet him, clearly he was here on some kind of official business. Indeed, the director had stood and was clearly expecting the policeman to join him.

"Upstart," Lord Atkinson said under his breath. "I'm going to find out what's afoot."

Diana bit her lip. She wouldn't stop him, but surely Director Quinn wouldn't take kindly to anyone interrupting his meeting. Not even a member of the nobility.

WHEN HE'D MADE HIS APPOINTMENT WITH SPACEPORT Security, Derek had hoped to be able to see the director of the spaceport. He was glad that, after he outlined the reasons for his visit, the main office agreed to send him upstairs to Director Quinn's office with a uniformed escort.

The fact that Derek might also encounter Diana had nothing to do with it, he told himself.

When the lift to the top of the spaceport dinged open,

however, she was the first thing he saw. She sat at a desk near the wide window, the light falling on her hair and illuminating the wisps escaping from her bun. Her dark gray dress was much more conservative than the ball gown he'd last seen her in, of course, but she still looked as poised and confident as ever.

Unfortunately, that arse Lord Atkinson was standing right by her. A bit too close, in Derek's opinion. As if feeling Derek's gaze, the nobleman glanced up and gave him a look of distaste.

Diana turned her chair about, plainly surprised to see him. He smiled at her, and her expression softened.

Derek showed his badge to the man at the entry desk. "I'm here to meet with the director. Officer Byrne, of the Southampton Police."

"Ah, yes. We received your message." The secretary indicated the gray-haired man rising from his work station at the end of the room. "Director Quinn is expecting you. Go ahead."

Derek nodded his thanks and strode forward. Much as he'd like to detour to say hello to Diana, he had business to attend to first.

To his irritation, Lord Atkinson straightened and stalked over. The two of them arrived at Director Quinn's desk at the same time.

"Yes, Lord Atkinson?" the director asked, his tone mild. "Is there something pressing you need me to attend to before I begin my meeting with Officer Byrne?"

The nobleman's nostrils flared. "I was interested to see what business brings the officer here."

"Police business," Derek said. "Nothing to trouble yourself over, my lord."

"I think perhaps I ought to hear it," Lord Atkinson said.

Director Quinn gave the man a quizzical glance. "Is there some reason in particular you feel you ought to be included, sir?"

For a moment, Lord Atkinson's gaze slipped to where Diana sat. Then he blinked and gave the director a bland smile. "If there are any safety concerns with the spaceport, shouldn't we all be informed?"

"There are no issues," Derek lied.

After all, a man seemingly affiliated with the galactic smugglers had ended up floating in the river. Even worse, of course, was the fact that Derek was there to gather information about the port's overall security, and the shipping schedules in particular. Which, not to put too fine a point on it, did constitute a rather large security breach.

"Thank you for your concern," Director Quinn said to Lord Atkinson. "If I'm in need of your counsel, I'll certainly inform you of the fact."

It was a clear dismissal. Derek could see the muscles bunching in his lordship's jaw as he made the director a curt nod.

"Very good," he said, then shot Derek a narrow-eyed gaze.

Damnú, was the fellow really that consumed with jealousy? Derek watched him stalk back toward Diana, feeling his own temper flare. She wasn't his, or anyone's, property. If she wanted to associate with Derek, that was her own business.

And though he might not like that she spent time with

Lord Atkinson, it wasn't up to him to dictate her acquaintances, either.

"Let us step into the conference room," Director Quinn said, shooting a quick glance at Lord Atkinson's retreating back.

"Fine with me," Derek said.

The director gestured him into the room, then followed, closing the door firmly behind them.

"Your message indicated this was concerning a murder?" Director Quinn asked, taking a seat and indicating that Derek do the same.

"Possibly." Derek explained about finding the body in the river and the subsequent translation of the text inside the ring that pointed to the galactic smuggler's association.

"That all seems rather troubling," the director said, one hand on his chin. "I can't say that I recall any violent incidents here at the spaceport around that time, but give me a moment and I'll call in one of my top security people. She might be able to shed more light on the situation. And would you care for a spot of tea? I find that a midmorning cup refreshes the mind."

"Surely." It was hardly an offer Derek could refuse.

The director's secretary appeared and nodded when he was instructed to send for the security officer. He reappeared after a short while with the tea tray and served them both bracing cups of strong black tea. When he disappeared again, Derek leaned forward.

"Do you mind my asking about how you met Miss Smythe?" he asked.

He'd heard Diana's side of the story, but she'd barely

told him enough to whet his curiosity. How, indeed, had she managed to change the arc of her life?

One of the director's brows rose. "Do you have a particular interest in the young lady?"

Derek felt the tips of his ears flush. "She and I are acquainted."

"Ah, from the streets, I suppose." The director nodded. "Yes, well, she and her young friend—the scrappy one, I see you know who I mean—managed to find an unsecured entrance into the spaceport."

"An unsecured entrance?" For a fleeting moment his pulse leaped. But no—security would have plugged that hole immediately. "How ever did they manage that?"

"Perseverance and luck. And indeed, it was lucky that Miss Smythe happened to be within the spaceport, at the right place and the right time to avert a crash that would have reflected badly on us." He shook his head. "Very, very badly."

"How did she stop it?" Derek asked.

"Miss Smythe possesses formidable mathematical abilities, and has an astonishing mind for spatial geometry. She was able to predict the trajectories of two ships as they ascended on a collision course, and begged Spaceport Security to intervene. Which, thanks to a sharp-witted guard, they did. Ah." Director Quinn looked up as the door opened and a woman dressed in the bright blue uniform of Spaceport Security came in. "In fact, here she is now. Good morning, Nails."

Derek swallowed his disappointment that he wouldn't get to hear more of Diana's story. It was now back to business.

"Director Quinn." The security guard nodded to him, then shot Derek a curious glance.

The director filled her in on the details of Derek's visit. When he had finished, Nails shook her head.

"Can't say there was anything amiss 'bout that time," she said. "We have our fair share of brawls and the like, but no bodies as I recall. Sorry I can't be of more help, officer."

"I think it might assist the station if you could send over the shipping schedules from last month," Derek said. "We can see if there's an irregularity in the pattern, perhaps."

The guard's brows pulled together. "That's confidential. We can't go sending those schedules about."

"Nails is correct," the director said. "Information about our ships' movements can't leave the port's secure system, I'm afraid."

Derek's mind worked furiously, even as he kept his expression bland.

"What if I came to the security office and took a quick look, then?" he said. "It shouldn't take long."

Director Quinn steepled his hands together. "That might suffice. Nails, if you'd accompany him?"

Relief flared through Derek. He'd be able to keep Diana out of his business with the INR.

"Thank you," he said. "There is one other thing." He pulled out his handheld and tapped to bring the image up. "Do you recognize this pattern? It was tattooed on the dead man's upper arm."

"Hm." Director Quinn leaned forward to study the triangle slashed through with three precise lines. "I'm afraid not."

"I think I may know it," Nails said.

Derek's attention veered to her. After so many dead ends, he was beyond ready for any possible lead. "Yes?"

"I've never clapped eyes on it, mind you," she said. "But I've heard that that symbol, or something like it, marks initiation into a dissident group opposing Queen Victoria's rule. Don't know which one, though, sorry to say."

"A smuggler *and* an anarchist?" Director Quinn's brows rose. "Your body sounds like quite the fellow. Good luck identifying him."

"Thank you." Derek's spirits dipped again.

There were any number of anti-Empire organizations riddling the galaxy. As he unfortunately knew all too well.

"Ready?" Nails said.

Derek gulped the last of his tea, then stood. "I appreciate your time, both of you. And, not to impose too greatly, but do you mind if I say hello to Miss Smythe on my way out?"

"By all means." Director Quinn waved his hand. "I'm glad she has friends such as you, Officer Byrne."

The praise made Derek squirm inside. But soon he'd have the information the INR wanted and then maybe, just maybe, he could be free of them.

I don't believe one's past controls one's future. Diana's words echoed through him. Could they possibly be true? Could he alter his own course without ending in a spectacular crash?

"I'll wait by the lift," Nails said.

As Derek strode to Diana's desk, Lord Atkinson stood, a scowl on his lips. Diana, however, rose, smiling,

"I was hoping you'd come over," she said, setting down

her pen in the middle of a notebook inscribed with equations. "Look at this view!"

He came to stand beside her, inhaling the clean scent of her as she described the ships coming in and out. It was a perfect vantage point, and, despite himself, he took note of the warehouses on the edge, the amount of traffic, and the best routes from the back entrance of the spaceport to the new construction area he'd spotted in the center.

"You sit here all day, watching?" he asked.

"Yes." She nodded at the shiny contraption on the corner of her desk. "I can speak to the control center using that. It's rather amazing." She pointed out the window. "See that area in the middle, undergoing construction? We've done quite a bit of streamlining, and on my advice the berths are being reclassified based on ignition and liftoff times."

"I'm working on a Calculations Device that does much the same," Lord Atkinson interrupted. "Based on Miss Smythe's brilliant work, of course."

"At any rate," Diana said, ignoring the nobleman, "I'm enjoying it very much."

"And I'm enjoying working with Miss Smythe." Lord Atkinson picked up a clockwork flower sitting on Diana's desk. "In fact, I gave her this just this morning as a token of my regard. As you might guess, it cost a pretty penny—but she's worth it."

"I personally don't believe in putting a price tag on my friendships," Derek said coldly.

Lord Atkinson set the flower down with a bump that made Diana wince. Derek hoped the delicate clockwork hadn't been damaged—though wouldn't that be an interesting metaphor for Lord Atkinson's *regard*?

"You're still coming to dinner tomorrow?" Diana asked.

"It would be my pleasure," Derek said, aware of the nobleman fuming beside them. "Six o'clock?"

"Perfect." She smiled. "I'd best get back to my work now, though."

"Of course."

Derek made Diana a bow, ignored Lord Atkinson altogether, and met Nails at the lift. He stepped inside, then couldn't help glancing once more at Diana. She was watching him, too—her smile cut off by the shining metal as the doors closed between them.

CHAPTER 19

Derek stood before the portico of Queensway Tower. Behind him, traffic flowed along the street, the clop of horses' hooves echoing the nervous beat of his pulse. He eyed his reflection in the tall entry doors, attempted to smooth back his hair, then rang the bell for Number 54.

The ornately grilled speaker beside the door crackled to life.

"Hello?" Diana said.

"It's Derek. I mean, Officer Byrne."

"I'll be right down." He could hear the smile in her voice. "Wait by the lift."

The door buzzed, releasing the lock, and he pushed through into the fancy lobby of the building. The place made his serviceable flat seem third-rate in comparison. What must the former streetrats think, living in such elegant surroundings?

An artful arrangement of roses sat in a cut crystal vase on a table in the center of the room, and Derek glanced down at the bouquet of wildflowers in his hand. On impulse, he'd bought the flowers from a girl at the train station selling hand-picked flowers from a dented tin bucket.

Bachelor buttons, sweet pea, bright field poppies, Queen Anne's lace—he knew the names from his childhood, and wondered if Diana did, too.

Now, though, his offering looked unkempt and out of place compared to the shining marble and gilt-framed mirrors around him. He glanced about for a bin, thinking to discard the flowers, but before he could do so, the lift arrived. Diana stepped out. She wore a white muslin dress that suited her, and her hair was caught in a braid over one shoulder, little wisps escaping from the sides.

Catching sight of him, she smiled. "Welcome to Queensway Tower. Oh, what a pretty bouquet."

Too late to toss away the flowers now. Derek held them out to her. "I hope you like them."

"I do, very much." She brought the colorful arrangement to her face and inhaled. "They smell wonderful, too."

"I think it's the sweet peas. My ma used to grow them."

He caught a waft of the scent, and for a moment vividly recalled the bright pink and white blossoms climbing up the old stone wall behind their cottage. Longing for home squeezed his heart. But though he couldn't return to that childhood cottage, perhaps he could find another place to belong.

"Come up." Diana set her fingers to the lift pad, and the doors dinged open again with a soft chime. "Tipper is working away in the kitchen."

The lift rose so smoothly, Derek could barely detect the

movement. The polished brass walls sent back wavery impressions of them, more blobs of color than anything.

"He's not planning to slip me poison, is he?" Derek asked.

She lifted one eyebrow in amusement. "You needn't worry. Tip isn't one to hold a grudge. Besides, you're my guest tonight, not an officer of the Southampton Police."

"Then I suppose you must call me Derek and not Officer Byrne."

"I suppose so."

He wished the lift might never arrive, so that he could stand there always, wreathed in the scent of flowers and the warmth of Diana's smile.

Then they arrived at the top floor, the doors whooshed open, and he berated himself for a sentimental fool.

The upper foyer was not quite as overwhelmingly grand as the one below. Derek's boots didn't ring as loudly over the parquet floors as they had on the marble, and there was no ostentatious bouquet to put his little posy to shame.

Diana opened the tall wooden door of Number 54 and ushered him in.

"You can hang your hat and overcoat here." She indicated a coat rack beside the door. "I'm just going to put these in water."

She waved the wildflowers at him and then disappeared into what he assumed was the kitchen. Derek took the opportunity to look about the sitting room. There was a plush rug on the floor, and the furnishings were elegantly nondescript. Likely they'd come with the flat.

However, the soft woolen scarf draped over one chair

arm and the cookery books piled haphazardly on the bookshelf gave the place a bit more personality. He was glad to see that Diana and Tipper seemed to be settling in well. If they could make a new life for themselves, then surely there was hope for him, too.

She beckoned to him from the kitchen doorway. "Come in and say hello to the chef."

He jammed his hands into his pockets, then took them back out and went to join Diana. Delicious scents wafted from the kitchen: garlic and fresh herbs. A cloud of steam greeted him. When it cleared, he saw Tipper at the sink, holding an empty pot over a colander of freshly cooked pasta.

"Hello, Tipper," Derek said, leaning against the door-jamb. "It smells good."

"Hope it tastes that way." The boy grinned at him. "Nice to see you, officer."

"We're going to call him Derek, this evening," Diana said. "Remember?"

Tipper wrinkled his nose at her. "I don't mind the fact he's a copper. Now that we're both on the right side of the law, aye?"

Derek swallowed back an admonishment to stay that way. He hoped Tipper would stay out of trouble, but lecturing him in his own kitchen would be rather rude. Derek could be blunt at times, but there were limits.

"Do you like seafood?" Diana asked, taking three plates down from the cupboard. "Tipper made Shrimp Scampi tonight, to impress you."

"Did not." The boy went to give a pan on the stove a stir.

"I like it very much," Derek said.

Diana set the plates on the counter, then turned to Derek. "What would you like to drink? We've wine, ale, water…"

"The ale's fresh from the tap at the White Oak tavern," Tipper said. "Not a bad brew."

"Ale it is, then." Derek glanced at the boy. "Are you a tippler now, in all your spare time?"

The boy winked at him. "Truth is, I spend every afternoon down at the pub."

"Only because you're working there," Diana said, a bit tartly. "Don't give Derek the wrong impression."

She'd used his name, which made Derek ridiculously happy.

"Washing dishes, is it?" he asked.

"Was." Tipper gave the pan another stir, then pulled it off the heat. "Now I'm apprentice to the cook. Di, grab the salad out?"

She opened the cooler and brought out a large bowl of greens decorated with sliced figs and dollops of some creamy white cheese.

"It looks delicious," Derek said.

"Sit, the both of you," Tipper said. "I'll bring your plates over."

Diana ushered him to the small table in the corner. His flowers were a splash of color, stuck into a pint glass, and looked perfectly at home in the cozy kitchen.

For the first half of the meal, they didn't say much, other than to praise Tipper's cooking. The boy shrugged, but Derek could tell he was pleased by the compliments. The boy clearly had more than a little talent in the kitchen.

On his second plate of shrimp, washed down with creamy brown ale, Derek told them the news from West Quay.

"Breggy's gone," he said. "We raided his den—thanks to you."

"Escaped, did he?" Tipper looked apprehensive at the thought.

"Not at all. His trial's just ended, and he's awaiting transportation on the next convict vessel going out."

"That would be the *Valiant*," Diana said. "An older Frauke, but a solid ship all the same. It's scheduled for blastoff on Monday. And I have to say, I'm glad to hear Breggy's gone for good."

Sadly, someone would rise soon enough to take the gangrunner's place, but Derek didn't want to dim the mood by saying so. Besides, both Diana and Tipper were streetwise. They knew well enough how things went in the slums.

After an extravagant dessert of chocolate cake with raspberries and whipped cream, they repaired to the sitting room. He sat by Diana on the couch, trying to keep a gentlemanly distance and yet all too aware of her proximity. Lamps glowed warmly on the end tables, and the sound of the night street below drifted up faintly; the hollow clop of horses' hooves, the occasional sound of a steam whistle warning pedestrians out of the way. Tipper flopped onto the floor, then groaned when Diana suggested she quiz him on his studies.

Apparently the boy had a tutor come in three days a week to teach him reading, mathematics and history. Diana asked him a variety of questions concerning Greek mythology. He answered them well enough, until she ventured into an area he didn't know. Face solemn, he fabricated absurd answers, and before long they were all laughing.

Still, the boy clearly was applying himself to his studies as well as his culinary explorations. If he kept it up, he'd go far, of that Derek had no doubt.

They used to say that about himself, he recalled with a twinge. His schoolmasters, friends of his Ma, everyone agreed that Derek had a bright future ahead.

But then his father had keeled over from strong drink and overwork, and Derek had taken his place at the factory. He'd thought that was bad enough—until the terrible day Seamus died and his life was spun into the gray fog.

"Are you feeling well, Derek?" Diana's soft voice broke into his bitter memories.

"Yes, sorry." He mustered up a smile. "Just a bit tired."

"Don't let us keep you." Concern shone from her clear eyes.

"It's not that." He cursed himself for implying he didn't want to be there any longer. "It's just this case I've been working on, with no luck."

"The one you were in Itchen about?"

He nodded, recalling that he'd asked her about the slashed triangle tattoo as they drank Turkish coffee together. It felt like years ago.

"Is that why you were at the spaceport?" she asked, ever perceptive.

"Yes, but I've hit a dead end there as well." He shrugged. "Sometimes cases never do get solved."

"That must be frustrating."

"I knew it was part of the job when I signed up."

"Why did you decide to be a copper?" Tipper asked, as though he could imagine no worse profession.

"I wanted to help people," Derek said.

Also, he'd been given no choice. The INR had threatened to expose his part in the bombing at the Irish Parliament—no matter that he'd been there to try and save his brother, and played a completely unwilling part in the terrorist act. Still, Derek's own guilt and horror at Seamus's death would haunt him to the end of his days. Though maybe working for the INR wasn't the answer to assuaging his guilt, after all.

He glanced at Diana. While it was true the past would never leave him, that didn't mean he had to serve it forever. She was beginning to show him the truth of it. Streetrat or lady, it didn't matter what you were. It mattered what you made of it.

"Well, you helped us." Diana reached over and touched his arm. "You even raided Breggy's because you thought we were there."

"That was brave." Tipper looked up at him, respect in his eyes.

"I didn't go by myself," Derek said. "Most of the Southampton force turned out."

He'd been one of the first in, though.

"Did they catch Pick?" Diana asked.

"Yes, and most of the other deputies. You needn't worry, Diana. You and Tipper are safe here."

I always settle my debts. Breggy's words echoed coldly in Derek's memory. But there was nothing the gangrunner could do to harm Diana now.

"We might be safe." Her voice was low. "But there are plenty more on the streets who aren't. I'm hoping to save up enough to help them, too."

"Aye." Tipper sat up straight. "Di's going to buy a ship and give streetrats free passage off Earth!"

"To where?" Derek asked.

It was a grand notion, but even leaving aside the prohibitive cost of buying a spaceship, he couldn't envision the orphans and urchins doing any better off-world than on. He hadn't been out into the galaxy, but it held the same squalor, the same divisions of rich and poor. Lives could be realigned, he was coming to believe that—but flying to the stars didn't change everything.

She pressed her lips together. "I'm still working it all out. There will have to be something for them to do, to live on, wherever they end up. And I'd need to find a colony that would take them in."

"New Eire might," he said, surprising himself.

It was true, though. His people had suffered enough that they knew what it was to starve, to be thought less than human. If anyone would take in a shipload of streetrats, it was the Irish.

Or the Quakers, but rumor was their world was already overflowing with refugees.

"There's a thought." Diana tilted her head at him. "New Eire's not full yet. And I hear it's in need of farmhands."

"I'm not going into the galaxy just to pull weeds," Tipper said, folding his arms.

She gave him an exasperated look. "Tip, there's plenty

more you could do. Cook, for one. But not everyone has your skills."

"You'd need a school," Derek said, her vision starting to come into focus for him. "Not just reading and writing, but trade skills, that sort of thing. A place where people could find their talents and then put them to good use."

"In between milking cows and the like?" A thoughtful expression crossed her face.

The sound of bells chiming the hour drifted up, and she glanced at Tipper.

"Eleven o'clock," she said. "Bedtime for you."

"But we have company." He gave her a pleading look.

"That's why you're still up. Be glad I didn't send you to bed at ten."

"I should be off." Derek rose. "Thank you for the delicious dinner. One of the best I've had all year."

"Really?" Tipper bounced to his feet, grinning. "Next time I'll make Duck a l'Orange, aye?"

"I'll see you out, Derek." Diana stood, then sent Tipper a stern look. "Get ready while I do."

"Of course. G'night, officer."

"Goodnight, Tipper."

Derek collected his hat and coat, and Diana wrapped the woolen shawl around her shoulders, then escorted him out the door.

"That was a fine evening," he said as they waited for the lift. Indeed, he'd enjoyed himself more than he'd imagined he could. A warm glow settled in his middle.

"It was. Thank you for coming." She looked at him, the light picking out golden streaks in her hair.

He lifted his hand to smooth the wayward strands, to

touch her face—he wasn't sure which. Before he could do either, the lift arrived with a bright chime. The doors whooshed open and they stepped inside. Suddenly, Derek felt as awkward as a schoolboy with his first infatuation.

As they descended, he stared at his boots, newly shined for the occasion, and wondered what to say. Surely he could think of something witty, or clever, or…

The arrived at the lobby. The smell of roses permeated the air as they silently walked to the doors.

"Well," he began, just as Diana began to speak.

They both broke off, and then she smiled.

"Do come again, Derek."

"I'd like that, very much." He halted just before the door. Then, before he could think too much, he bent to kiss her.

Their lips brushed, the softest touch, and his heartbeat pounded through him. She didn't pull away, but instead breathed a soft *oh*, her breath warm on his skin.

Too much, too close. Too perfect—and he wasn't ready for anything nearly so close to heaven.

"Goodnight, Diana," he said, pulling back.

She simply gazed up at him, then put her fingers to her lips.

Damnú, if he stayed there any longer, he'd kiss her again. And again. But he wasn't free yet. He needed to finish his business with the INR. Only then would he be able to meet Diana, openhearted, to see what they could make of their lives—together.

The sound of his own wanting loud in his ears, he made her a quick bow, and fled out into the night.

CHAPTER 20

WHEN THE DOORBELL RANG THE NEXT DAY, DIANA JUMPED up to answer it. To her regret, it wasn't Derek's voice, but Lord Atkinson's issuing from the speaker.

"Good afternoon, Diana," he said. "I was hoping I might tempt you to go for a drive in the park."

Her first impulse was to send him away—but then she'd only sit on the sofa, wrestling with the turmoil of her feelings. So far, she'd nothing to show for it but a cup of cold tea and a lingering sense of melancholy.

The equations of her heart were not adding up satisfactorily, no matter how she tried to balance them. On one side were all the reasons love was an unreliable, unquantifiable emotion, too weak a force to have a lasting effect on the universe. And on the other side was… Derek Byrne.

By all the stars, she wished the human heart was not so complicated.

In addition to the algebra of her own emotions, she was left trying to calculate how he felt about her in return. It seemed he cared for her, if that kiss was any indication. That kiss… She set her fingers to her lips and sighed.

Then gave herself a sharp mental shake. She should be grateful Lord Atkinson had arrived and given her a reason to bestir herself. Perhaps she could pluck a daisy while she was out. The flower's predictive powers were probably just as accurate as her own theories. *He loves me. He loves me not.*

"I'd enjoy that, Lord Atkinson," she said into the speaking tube. "Give me a few moments to get ready."

"Certainly." He sounded pleased. "I'll be waiting at your convenience."

She went and changed from her dressing gown into her favorite blue-gray dress, tucking a few bills into the corset, just in case. Tipper was down at the White Owl, so she jotted him a quick note saying she was out and not to wait supper for her.

Likely she'd be home by then, but perhaps Lord Atkinson was planning a picnic. She pinned her hat on over her upswept bun, collected her gloves and reticule, and went down to meet him

Stepping outside, she was glad to see Lord Atkinson waiting in an elegant two-person barouche—no footman, no driver, no ostentatiously decorated carriage. He tied off the reins, then jumped down to assist her.

A twinge of annoyance went through her. Yes, it was polite and gentlemanly of him, but she could climb into the vehicle by herself—though it would be easier if she were wearing trousers instead of skirts. She rarely felt nostalgic for her time on the streets. But the way Society, and the gentry in particular, treated ladies was a bit absurd.

"Good afternoon, Diana." Lord Atkinson offered her his hand. "Thank you for joining me on this lovely day."

She let him settle her into the passenger side. The horse —a white mare—stood quietly as he returned to his seat and took up the reins.

"I'm glad you stopped by," she said, though she didn't tell him why. "Where are we going?"

"There's a fine drive along the greensward," he said. "Have you ever visited the tower folly in East Park?"

"I haven't." The only parts of Southampton she knew at all were the slums of West Quay and the train line leading from Queensway to the spaceport.

As he steered them expertly through the traffic, he kept the conversation light and amusing. The sun filtered through the branches of the tall trees they drove beneath, and Diana was, quite frankly, glad of the distraction.

She was careful not to bring up his Calculations Device, or Derek, or anything that might sour the mood.

After a half an hour, Lord Atkinson steered the barouche off the main drive and onto a lane leading away through the park. Beyond the manicured green lawns lay unmowed fields where wildflowers grew in bright profusion, and she smiled to see the poppies and bright blue bachelor's buttons. Unfortunately—or perhaps fortunately —there were no daisies in evidence.

"It feels like we're out in the country," she said.

The air was quiet, even the ever-present sound of ships blasting off from the spaceport muted. As if sensing her thoughts, Lord Atkinson glanced into the clear blue sky.

"This is the first weekend that Director Quinn has

allowed my device to be hooked up with the control center," he said.

Diana nodded. She was aware of the fact, but hadn't wanted to say anything unless he mentioned it first.

"I'm sure it will do a fine job," she said.

"Of course it will." He shot her an irritated look. "It's been perfectly functional for the last week, but the director didn't want to test it until now."

"Perhaps he didn't want to pay you for the privilege," she said dryly.

It had surprised her to learn that Lord Atkinson intended to charge the spaceport for use of his device. Then Nails had confided that, in general, the nobility were quite poor. Centuries of maintaining a certain standard of living, coupled with a disdain for actual work, had ruined the fortunes of many noble houses. Lord Atkinson's financial situation was, Diana gathered, rather worse than she'd guessed.

He gave her a haughty look. "The fee for making use of my Calculations Device costs the spaceport far less than paying your salary, Miss Smythe."

Well. There wasn't anything she could say to that.

They rode along in stiff silence for a few minutes. Ahead, Diana could see the round shape of a tower rising slightly above the trees and fields.

"I'm sorry." Lord Atkinson reached over and took her hand. "You might not believe me, but I am not usually so contentious. There's something about you, Diana, that brings out the fire in me."

She would call it rudeness, not fire. But there was no

point in arguing, since they still were working together. Or were they? She shot him a glance.

"With your device completed, I suppose I won't be seeing as much of you," she said. And thank heavens for that.

"Perhaps not. Ah, but here we are."

He pulled the barouche to a stop outside the tower. Swallows darted in the air above the sun-warmed stones, and a climbing rosebush decorated the walls, small pink flowers shedding their petals on the ground below. Before Lord Atkinson could come around to assist her out of the vehicle, Diana hopped down.

She bent to smooth her skirts, and hide her smile at the look of annoyance on his face. Truly, she shouldn't enjoy aggravating him so much, but pulling his tail seemed to be something she excelled at. It would be a pity to stop now.

"Shall we go inside?" He held out an arm.

She glanced at the arched doorway leading into the shadows. Dimly, she could make out a flight of ruined stairs spiraling up the inner walls.

"It is safe?"

"Of course. We won't go up, but I'm told this is considered a very romantic spot."

A flash of alarm went through her and she gave him a sharp glance. Did Lord Atkinson really believe he was courting her? She settled her fingertips on his arm, ready to dash away the moment he began to make any protestations of love.

They had to duck beneath a spray of roses as they entered, and once inside the tower, Diana had to admit it held a certain musty charm. Sunbeams filtered overhead, and the rose vines twined with ivy partway down the walls, giving it a bower-like feeling.

"Diana." Before she knew what he was about, Lord Atkinson took her by the shoulders and gazed intently into her eyes. "I hope you know that I've come to respect you, despite your unfortunate past—and I do regret this. But I have no choice."

Her thoughts crashed to a halt, and she stared up at him.

"What are you saying? Ow!" She jerked away at the sharp pinch to her arm, to see that he'd just injected her with a needle of some kind.

Run! her mind screamed. She turned, trying to sprint away, but all she managed was a few stumbling steps toward the door.

"Yes, out we go." He set his hand at her back and pushed her forward. "You'll need to climb into the carriage before you lose consciousness entirely."

"Why?" Her tongue felt slow and heavy in her mouth. "What have you done to me?"

The trailing rosebushes caught on her hat, and she batted at them ineffectually with arms made of lead. It was too difficult, and she simply wanted to sink down and sit for a while…

"No, no, you must keep going." Lord Atkinson hauled her to the barouche. "Do understand, it's not personal, my dear, only necessary. Onto the step now, up you go."

He shoved her upward, and she fell into the barouche, sprawling across the seat. In a moment he was there, wrapping a blanket about her and then propping her against him. Her head lolled back against his shoulder and she knew she ought to do something. Kick him, or scream, or… but the sky was so blue.

"Rayleigh scattering," she mumbled. "Inversely proportional… fourth power wavelength…"

Behind the sky was the dark of space.

Behind her eyelids more of the same, though that darkness held no stars. Only black.

CHAPTER 21

DEREK TOOK A LONG SWALLOW OF HIS MORNING TEA, TRYING to prod his sluggish brain into waking. He'd lain in his bed far too long the night before, unsleeping, thinking of Diana. Thinking of his past, and of his future.

Time for him to be done with the first, and move onward into the second. Time to make that small adjustment that would ultimately deliver him to a new destination. Today.

His decision made, Derek took a deep breath and pushed back from the rickety table in his two-room flat. It didn't take long for him to do the washing up, and then pull on his coat and boots and run a comb through his hair.

Half an hour later he was strolling through Southampton's fish market, a sprig of greenery tucked into his breast pocket. It was the signal he'd been told to use if he needed the INR to make contact.

To extend his time there without seeming suspicious, he bought a packet of fish and chips from one of the vendors. Leaning against a piling, he ate them slowly and watched the light dance off the water. It was mesmerizing, the way the sparkles ran up and down the edges of the ripples, and he felt a deep quiet enter his soul.

Not sure how long he should linger in the market, he meandered between the stalls and finally purchased a small flounder to fry up for his supper. Fish twice in one day wasn't his preference, but it was necessary.

In truth, he'd eat fish every day for a month if it meant he'd be free of the INR at last.

He hadn't realized how much his double identity weighed on him, until the prospect of ending the charade was lifted from his shoulders. Perhaps that heaviness was why it had taken him so long to do the resistance's bidding. They certainly hadn't been pleased with his performance thus far.

And what of his debt to Seamus? He wrestled with that question as he strode the wharf, the smell of tar wafting up from the boards. Would his brother really want Derek to give up his future, for a blood debt he'd placed on himself? Was Derek willing to do so?

No.

He was not fit for a life of subterfuge. Not even in service to his country. As soon as Molly contacted him—which he hoped would be soon—he'd tell her what he'd discovered about the spaceport and its shipping schedules, and then be done with the INR.

Not done with being a constable, however, he realized to his own surprise. Despite the flaws in the system, he believed he could continue to do some good if he remained a policeman. And he welcomed the thought of being a respectable officer with a clear conscience, who might court a certain young lady in the employ of the spaceport, without any lies between them.

Derek was not surprised to find that his feet had turned him up Queensway, toward the tallest of the buildings set along the busy avenue.

And why not visit Diana? He glanced down at the wrapped fish in his string shopping bag. It wasn't the best courting gift, he had to admit. Perhaps Tipper would like the flounder. No doubt the boy would be able to cook it up in a tasty manner.

Whistling a tune from his childhood, Derek strode up to the entryway of the tower and pressed the bell for Number 54.

Only silence greeted him.

He tried again, and then, after waiting several minutes, once more. There was no reply, and for some reason anxiety fell across his mood, like a cloud shadowing the sun.

Where could they be?

Any number of places, you fool, he told himself. Likely they were out shopping, just as he was.

Speaking of which, he ought to get his fish home before it started to turn in the warm summer day. Derek shot a last glance at the top story of the Queensway Tower, then, shaking the foreboding from his shoulders, started for home.

"Message for you," Cribbs said as Derek came into the station early Monday morning.

Derek tried not to snatch the piece of paper from the man's hand. *Damnú*, the last twenty-four hours had felt like a year. A dozen times he'd thought of going to visit Diana, but hadn't wanted to leave his flat, just in case a message came.

Of course, nothing had.

Still, he wanted to be done with the INR before he saw her again. One thing at a time, no matter how impatience gnawed at his bones.

Forcing his expression to remain calm, Derek unfolded the note. Of course, Cribbs had certainly read it, and whoever had brought the missive, and who knows who else.

Fountain even, was the only thing it said.

Derek knew exactly what that meant. Meet at the Bargate drinking fountain at the top of any even hour. He gave his pocket watch a quick glance. The hour was just rising eight. If he hurried, he could be there in time to meet his contact.

"Well?" Cribbs gave him a tired look.

"I'm off to meet an informant," Derek said. "I'll be back as soon as I can."

The older policeman just pursed his lips and gave a nod. Ever since Derek had instigated the raid on Breggy's hideout, the other officers had treated him with more respect. It was a welcome change.

Back out into the slanted sunbeams of morning, Derek hastened to the oldest part of the city. The cobblestones seemed cleaner in the freshness of a new day, but not as light as his heart felt. Just as the cathedral bells tolled out the hour, he arrived at the carved stone urn where water splashed down into a shallow pool.

And there, to his relief, was Molly, carrying a basket of onions, her red hair ablaze in the sunshine. She caught his eye and jerked her head toward one of the alleyways leading to the fountain square. Without waiting for his acknowledgement, she strode away in the opposite direction.

Derek went clockwise around the square, trying to look as if he were simply on his rounds. When he reached the shadowed alley, he stepped inside.

"There you are," Molly said, setting down her basket. She sounded as though she'd been waiting for hours for him to appear, instead of the other way around.

"I have information for you," he said, keeping his voice low.

"Praise all the stars. And high time, too. We were beginning to lose faith in you, Derek Byrne. Tell me what you know."

Tersely, described what he'd seen of the shipping schedules, then told her about the new construction in the middle of the spaceport.

"Perfect." Her eyes were glowing with approval. "Just in time for the Queen's Ruby Jubilee next weekend. We'll give those bloody English a show to remember, aye."

"Wait." He held up his hand, his throat suddenly tight with apprehension. "What do you mean, a show? I thought you were going to smuggle out fugitives."

"Oh, Derek. That was our plan months ago, but things have changed. The INR must make a statement, a show of rebellion—and what could be better than the fortieth anniversary of the false queen's reign?"

Understanding filtered through him, followed by despair. Dear heaven, what had he just done?

"You mean to bomb the spaceport," he said. The words tasted like metal in his mouth. Like death.

"Of course."

The bitter truth lay between them, and he wanted to grab handfuls of his hair and rip it from his own scalp for not guessing at it sooner. No matter what they said, the INR had been planning violence all along. His lungs felt full of salt, the air barely able to rasp through the sharp edges of that betrayal. And his own gullability.

Molly gave him a scornful look. "You're as soft as they say, Derek. But don't think to go running to the *real* constables about this. After all, you're the one who infiltrated the spaceport and brought us the information. If you try to bring the INR down, you'll come along with us. Understand?"

He clenched his jaw, nauseated by what had happened. And what was to come. The memory of the explosion at the Irish Parliament filled his senses: the acrid smoke burning his lungs, the screams of panic mixing with the cries of the injured into an unbearable cacophony.

And moments before the bomb went off, Seamus kneeling on the pavement, his gaze meeting Derek's as he lit the fuse and let it go.

"Very well." Derek choked out the words. "For the sake of my brother, I'll do what has to be done."

"Good." Her smile was hard. "I knew we could count on you. Even if that information was a long time coming."

May his soul burn in the fiery depths of the sun for it, too.

"I'd best return to West Quay," he said, his voice stilted. "Don't want anyone getting suspicious."

"Aye, for now it's business as usual." She bent and scooped up her basket of onions. "Meet me here again on Thursday, same time, and you'll be given further instructions."

He managed a tight nod, while inside his soul was screaming.

"And Derek," she said, her voice low and full of threat, "make no mistake. We'll be watching you."

CHAPTER 22

Diana woke, head aching, in a hard, narrow bed. The air held the tang of rusty metal. A hollow clanking noise sounded at regular intervals, making her wince.

Where in all the bright stars was she?

Carefully, she sat up, then sucked in a dismayed breath to discover she was in a cell. Thick iron bars made up three walls, with solid metal at her back. The cot she sat on was bolted to the stained concrete floor.

That villain Lord Atkinson had done this to her, curse his black soul. At least she was alive, though her prospects didn't seem very promising at the moment.

The woman in the next cell over leaned against the bars and gave her a gap-toothed grin. "Welcome to paradise, luv."

Diana folded her arms, wishing she was wearing her torn trousers, with her hair bundled under her cap. A corset and skirts were a liability in a fight—and fight she would.

The other woman reached a dirty hand out of the bars

and beckoned to a bored-looking guard standing watch at the end of the corridor.

"Oi," she called. "Her ladyship's awake. Tell Breggy."

Breggy? Diana's blood chilled. Oh, she was in deeper trouble than she'd guessed.

The only good thing about that bit of information was she now knew where she was—imprisoned in the bowels of the transport ship *Valiant*. She could think of no worse place she could possibly be.

Unless it was lying with her throat slit in the folly tower of East Park.

She supposed she should be glad of that much—that Lord Atkinson, despite his utter lack of empathy, had only kidnapped her. Likely he wanted to keep his hands clean. Murder was such a messy business.

The thud of boot heels against metal made her rise. She didn't want to face Breggy sitting down. Bracing herself against a wave of dizziness, she went to stand near the bars. She chose a place where she could see down the corridor but was still out of reach of anyone trying to take a swipe at her.

Breggy came into view. Despite the fact he wore a stun cuff and was accompanied by two guards, he swaggered down the corridor as if he owned it. And perhaps he did, if he had free run of the ship.

"Well, well." He stopped in front of her cell and smiled, his gold tooth glinting. "If it isn't our old friend Diver. Come up a bit in the world, haven't you, *miss*? And then down again, clearly."

He swept his hand out, indicating the rows of cells.

"Hello, Breggy," she said warily. There was no use denying who she was.

"Turns out, we have a few acquaintances in common." He sauntered up to the bars. Despite his smile, his eyes were as cold as sleet. "Officer Byrne paid me a visit, along with most of the constabulary of Southampton. He was looking for you."

She made no response, and his expression hardened.

"The thing I'd like to know, is how did he find me?" Breggy leaned forward, menace in his stance. "I heard that a certain streetrat blabbed something they shouldn't have. And believe me, she'll pay."

He lifted his fist in a sudden, violent motion. Diana flinched, but stood her ground. The gangrunner wanted to see her cringe away, but she wouldn't give him the satisfaction.

Didn't mean she wasn't in for a beating later, of course. Girl or no, Breggy doled his punishments out evenly.

She couldn't check to see if the banknotes were still hidden in her corset, but if they were, at least she had something she could use to her advantage.

Not with Breggy, though—that was clear by the unforgiving light in his eyes. But maybe one of the guards could be bribed. She'd have to try. Later.

"Let me go," she said, knowing it was hopeless.

"I don't think so." He leaned up against the bars of her cell. "I had to call in more than a few favors to get you here."

"Lord Atkinson?" It was a guess, but not a wild one. After all, it was fairly clear that the nobleman had been the one to drug and deliver her to the *Valiant*.

The gangrunner flashed his gold smile at her. "Always were a clever one, Di. Yes, a few years back the poor lordling was having some difficulty with his inheritance. Said difficulty being his older brother. Nothing a bit of a runaway carriage couldn't solve, however."

Dear stars, Lord Atkinson had arranged to have his older brother murdered so that he could inherit?

The answer was plain enough. She supposed the rest of it would be, too, given a little thought. Breggy clearly had more connections, both high and low, than she'd ever suspected, and somehow her links to the spaceport, and Lord Atkinson, had been ferreted out. And turned to the gangrunner's advantage.

Biting down on the questions crowding her throat, she settled for staring wordlessly at his shoulder. Best not to meet his eyes.

He let out a *tsk*. "Nothing else to say? Don't worry, we'll have plenty of time to renew our old acquaintance."

The promise of violence beneath his words made her shiver.

CHAPTER 23

Derek spent the next few hours trying not to choke on the knowledge of what he'd done.

At least he still had time to warn the spaceport, and Diana, of the planned attack. He must tread carefully, though. If Molly suspected his intent, he'd no doubt she'd cosh him over the head and drag him off somewhere to keep him from interfering with the INR's plans.

And so he went through the motions of his deskwork, his heart a pile of ashes in his chest.

All the bright hope he'd nurtured, burned away to nothing. Diana had been wrong. There was no changing the future. But this time, he vowed, he'd give his life to keep the past from repeating itself. To save her, and the spaceport, no matter the cost.

A small figure barged through the station doors, interrupting his grim thoughts. Derek was on his feet in an instant, one hand going to his stunclub.

"Tipper?" He blinked. The West Quay station was the last place he'd ever expect to see the boy again.

"Where's Di?" Tipper demanded. His shirt was untucked, his hair disheveled.

"I've no idea." The despair that had been eddying around Derek rose in a wave.

"You don't?" The boy's eyes widened with fear. "She didn't come home at all last night. And then Nails came by this morning to see if she was unwell, since she hadn't gone to work, and sent no word."

No. Derek couldn't lose everything in the space of a single day. Not again.

"When was the last time you saw Diana?"

"Yesterday, 'fore I went down to the pub. When I came home, she'd left a note saying she'd gone out, and not to expect her for dinner. I figured she'd went to see you and, well, spent the night."

If only that had been true.

"We're going to the spaceport," Derek said, grabbing his overcoat. "Maybe she's there, after all, just delayed."

And if she wasn't? His breath seized in his chest. Then he'd find her. He had to.

"I'm sorry," Director Quinn said. "I've no idea where Miss Smythe might be. Nails has already reported that she wasn't at home."

Derek stood before the director's desk, Tipper at his side, and felt his blood turn to iron in his veins.

"What's that, you say?" Lord Atkinson rose from his desk, where a device in a large metal box was clicking away. "Miss Smythe has disappeared?"

"So it seems," the director said.

Derek rounded on the nobleman. "Do you have any idea where she is?"

"Me? Why should I keep track of a former streetrat?" Lord Atkinson blinked at him. "Are you certain she didn't decide she liked her old life better?"

"She'd never." Tipper balled his hands into fists and lunged at the man, but Derek caught him by the collar.

"Steady on," he told the boy, though he was in complete agreement with Tipper's reaction.

Derek looked back at Lord Atkinson, noting the faint evidence of scratches on the man's jaw, the insincere smile on his lips. Suspicion blew over him like a cold breeze, the intuition he'd always been able to rely on.

"What are you working on, there?" He nodded to the desk.

"It's my Calculations Device. Good thing it's operational, since Miss Smythe seems to have deserted her duty."

"It's taking over for her? How convenient." Derek ambled toward the desk, keeping his hands relaxed at his sides.

"Not that Miss Smythe is replaceable," the director said, "but the device does an adequate job."

Derek reached the machine and glanced at the strip of paper feeding out.

:PRIORITY: Approve VALIANT for liftoff earliest possible slot:

The name sounded familiar, and he searched his memory. Right—the convict transport Diana had mentioned. Suspicion squeezing his gut, he glanced at Lord Atkinson.

"What's the *Valiant*?" Derek asked, his tone casual despite the edge of panic pulsing through him.

"Supply ship, I believe." Lord Atkinson's gaze slipped away from his. "Grain to Blue Crumpet."

He was lying. Diana was gone, and the nobleman seemed to have prepared for her disappearance. It added up to an ugly picture.

Without waiting another second, Derek strode to the communications device on the corner of Diana's desk. He toggled it on, then lifted the microphone.

"Hello, control?" he asked.

"Yes." The voice on the other end of the line confirmed the connection.

"This is Director Quinn's office. Immediate abort of the *Valiant*'s liftoff. I repeat, immediate—"

The communicator went flying as Lord Atkinson tackled Derek.

"Let it go," the nobleman said, fingers scrabbling for Derek's throat. "Damned interfering–"

His breath escaped with a whoosh as Derek jammed his knee into his stomach. As Lord Atkinson lay there gasping, Derek got to his feet. Then, for good measure, he slapped a cuff on the man.

A tinny voice emerged from the speaker. "Sir? Hello, sir? I'm sorry, but the *Valiant* has already taken off."

No.

Derek rushed to the window, splaying his hands over the glass. A large ship was lumbering into the air, engines firing. It rose, secondary boosters sending it rapidly into the stratosphere as he watched helplessly.

Breggy was on that transport.

And, unless Derek was very much mistaken, so was Diana.

~

A WARNING CLAXON SOUNDED THROUGH THE *VALIANT*, AND the guard next to Breggy jerked his head. "Time to go. We're preparing for liftoff."

"Right." Breggy said. He gave Diana one last look, the way a cat regards a trapped mouse. "We're not done, Diver —not by any stretch. So you just bide on that in your cell. By the time we reach Halgrek, I'm sure we'll manage any number of suitable punishments."

She didn't look away, didn't let the fear pounding through her show on her face. It wasn't until Breggy sauntered back down the corridor, escorted by the two guards, that she let out the breath she'd been holding and sagged weakly against the bars.

Despair pressed at her until she could scarcely take the weight. Could scarcely breathe past the fact that everything had, once again, changed irrevocably.

And for the very, very worse.

This was her new life now; transportation to the prison world of Halgrek, on a ship full of hardened criminals and a gangrunner determined to inflict as much pain on her as possible. If Breggy didn't kill her, the other prisoners or the harsh conditions in the ice mines would.

The floor beneath her feet thrummed as the engines ignited, and her breath caught in her throat. No escape, now.

"All hands, strap down for liftoff," a sharp-edged voice

announced through the comm system. "Prisoners, secure yourselves to your bunks."

Diana stumbled back to her cot. Lying down, she pulled the shock webbing over herself and hooked it onto the other side. It would be adequate, she supposed. And if any of the prisoners didn't strap in properly and were injured during takeoff, they were no doubt considered expendable.

The ship shuddered, then lurched up, the sturdy Frauke straining against gravity. Diana closed her eyes, imagining Director Quinn standing at the viewing window.

I'm here! she wanted to shout. But no one would hear. No one would know where she'd gone, or what fate she was bound for.

As the ship rose, the vibrations juddering through her bones, she imagined Southampton falling away beneath. Nails, striding the gleaming corridors of the spaceport. Tipper, stirring a pot of stew in the kitchen of the White Owl. And Derek, walking the streets of West Quay.

All of them would look up as the ship she was on blasted away, out of Earth's orbit. None of them would ever guess that she was on board, being taken away from them. Forever.

The force of the *Valiant*'s acceleration pushed down hard on her chest. She could barely breathe as hot tears leaked out of the corners of her eyes. As her past once more burned to ashes behind her.

"WE HAVE TO GO AFTER THAT SHIP," DEREK SAID, HIS CHEST tight as he watched the *Valiant* disappear into the blue.

"Hurry," Tipper whispered, slipping his small hand into Derek's.

Derek squeezed it, then turned to the director. Despite the clamor of his thoughts, he forced his breathing to slow, forced himself not to scream at the man to do something. Anything.

"Spaceport Security is already after them," Director Quinn said. "And my personal transport is being prepped for liftoff. Come."

"What about him?" Derek nodded to Lord Atkinson, who had slowly risen to his feet.

"Me?" The nobleman shot Derek a glare and began sidling toward the lift. "I'm bringing charges against you for assault."

"Will that be before, or after, your trial for kidnapping?" Derek asked coldly.

Lord Atkinson's only answer was to turn and bolt for

the exit. Unfortunately for him, a trio of blue-uniformed security guards burst out of the lift, just as Derek activated the stun cuff.

The nobleman fell to the ground, writhing, while the guards surrounded him. Silently, Derek handed the cuff control to Nails, who had led the charge.

Director Quinn pointed to Lord Atkinson. "Guards, take that man into custody. Nails, you're with me. We'll sort out the rest of this when we return. Le, you're in charge."

The secretary stood up from behind his desk, his face pale. "Very good, sir."

To Derek's surprise, instead of heading for the lift, Director Quinn led them to the back of the suite. He pressed one of the carved panels on the wall, which swung open to reveal a hidden elevator.

"It's an indulgence," the director said, "but in this case, a very useful one."

The four of them—Derek, Tipper, the director, and Nails—crammed into the small space.

"It'll be good to have two of you with combat experience," Director Quinn said. "Just in case."

"Can we catch up to the *Valiant*?" Tipper asked, looking up at the director.

"Yes. My personal ship is faster than nearly any other craft. We can certainly reach the *Valiant* before the Yxleti Drive kicks in and boosts them light years away."

The lift doors slid open, and the director led them into a private hangar. A blade-shaped silver ship sat in the middle of the floor, crew members bustling about it.

"It don't look very big," Tipper said, eyeing the vessel.

"Her name is the *Vesper*, and she's big enough," Director Quinn said. "Will you sit up front and help me navigate?"

"You're piloting?" Derek asked, glancing at the gray-haired man and trying to keep his doubts to himself.

"Haven't you heard of Quantum Quinn?" Nails raised her brows at him. "The director might not be flying the space routes in record time any more, but he's still one of the best pilots in the galaxy."

"Thank you for that, Nails. I still get my hours in, as I can." The director ducked through an oblong hatch into the belly of the ship. "Tipper, with me. Nails and Officer Byrne, grab a seat and strap in."

There were only three chairs to choose from, set in an area just behind the round-windowed pilot's bay. Derek took the one on the left, while Nails settled in the middle. Up front, Director Quinn helped Tipper buckle in, then pulled on a pair of goggles, perching them high atop his head.

"Helps me see the displays once we get out into the starlight," he said, strapping in with the ease of long familiarity. "Ready?"

Derek nodded, his fingers tight around the armrests. He hadn't imagined his first time out into space would be like this. To be honest, he hadn't really imagined it at all. His path had been to atone for his past and fight for Ireland—not to leap off the planet in a tiny metal ship in pursuit of the woman he loved.

The hangar doors opened, letting in the bright light of day.

"Here we go." Director Quinn flipped a few switches, and the ship roared to life.

It felt to Derek as though the engine was located right under his feet, vibrating up through the soles of his boots. Before he could take another breath, the *Vesper* shot out, then up. In the cockpit, Tipper squealed with delight, but Derek felt like he'd left his stomach somewhere in the vicinity of West Quay.

Director Quinn was steering, saying something to Tipper, but Derek couldn't hear them over the noise of launch. The sky was white, then blue, then darkest indigo. He pulled in a shuddering breath. Only a thin metal skin between himself and the nothing.

Beside him, Nails shot him a sympathetic glance. "First time up?"

He managed a nod.

"It gets easier. Try watching the stars."

He faced forward, trying to focus on the pinpricks of light shining in the black. A silver coin quickly grew into the shape of the moon. Before he could fathom it, they'd zipped past. Mars, red and round, floated like some child's lost ball off to their right.

"We'll catch them around Jupiter," the director called. "I'm radioing the *Valiant* now to prepare for a boarding party."

"Are you sure it's wise to go in, sir?" Nails asked.

Director Quinn shot her a glance over his shoulder. "What other choice do we have?"

There was no answer to that.

Derek swallowed. What if he'd been wrong? What if Diana wasn't on board, and this pursuit was for nothing?

What if she was lost to him, forever? He felt like ripping his heart out of his chest and sending it spinning into the darkness outside. It might be less painful than allowing it to continue beating beneath his ribs.

"I see 'em." Tipper leaned forward, pointing to something shining ahead.

Bigger than a star, and getting rapidly larger. The director's hands were busy on the controls, and the *Vesper's* vibration slowed.

"Not easy, docking in space," he said. "Have to match the velocities point on."

Diana would be good at that, Derek thought, his gaze fastened on the bulk of the *Valiant*.

Slowly, too slowly for his taste, their ship crept abreast of the transport. Then they were there, hovering what felt like a hand's breadth above the mottled exterior. The director nosed the *Vesper* over the pitted surface, then dropped them down with a lurch.

Derek nearly choked on his fear before he realized they'd entered a docking bay. The clang of the bay doors closing reverberated like thunder as Director Quinn landed his ship with a soft thump inside the *Valiant*.

"That was a grand flight." Tipper's grin was the widest Derek had ever seen.

"They tried to refuse us entry," Director Quinn said, glancing over his shoulder. "I used my authority to override. But be on the lookout for anything suspicious."

"Can we get out now and find Di?" Tipper asked.

"Give them a moment to reestablish the atmosphere," the director said. "They'll signal when it's safe to disembark."

Derek unbuckled the straps holding him securely to the chair, and was glad to find that his legs supported him when he went to stand. Beside him, Nails gave him a wry look.

"All right?" she asked.

"Aye."

A sharp signal echoed through the hangar, and Director Quinn went to release the hatch. He slipped out, with Tipper right behind him. Derek followed, one hand on his stunclub. Whatever trouble lay ahead, he was determined to extract Diana from the *Valiant*. Even if he had to fight the entire British Galactic Army to do so.

CHAPTER 25

THE SOUND OF FOOTSTEPS THUDDING DOWN THE CORRIDOR brought Diana upright. After the turbulence of liftoff had faded, she'd lain in the cot, trying to imagine her way forward. No matter how much she turned the possibilities about, she feared only shadows and fog lay ahead.

And Breggy.

Though he wasn't accompanying the red-coated guards now approaching her cell.

"You there." The taller of the two redcoats beckoned to her. "Smythe, is it?"

There was no point in denying her name. "Yes."

"You're to come with us."

Her lungs squeezed tight. Breggy was moving even more quickly than she'd anticipated. At least she'd pulled the banknotes from her corset and put them someplace more reachable. In addition, she'd worked one of the metal corset stays free and stuck it down the side of her boot.

As weapons went, it wasn't much, but it would do. Much like the makeshift knife she'd left in her bolthole in

204

West Quay. Not terribly deadly, but just knowing she had it helped steady her nerves.

The taller guard unlocked her cell. "Come on, then," he said.

When she stepped out, he grabbed her elbow. She was surprised they didn't stun cuff her. Was she really perceived as that little of a threat? The thin piece of metal in her boot jabbed against her ankle.

As soon as they rounded the corner and were out of sight of the cells, she halted.

The guard holding her tugged her forward. "We've no time for this."

"I've got money," she said, pulling the banknotes from her sleeve. "All I'm asking is a few minutes at a comm. Or someone to send a message for me. Please."

The guard shook his head. "No need for that, miss. We're taking you to see the colonel."

By all the stars, had Breggy already corrupted the commander of the *Valiant*? The taste of fear was sour in her mouth.

To her surprise, they escorted her to a bustling control room beside what looked like a hangar inside the ship. A man with several shiny medals pinned on his scarlet coat straightened from the control panel and gave her a piercing look.

"Miss Diana Smythe?" he asked.

"Yes."

"I'm Colonel Blake." He looked her up and down. "Excellent—you're unharmed. We were informed you were on board as a victim of kidnapping."

Her knees went weak with relief and she grabbed the

back of a nearby chair for support. They'd found her. Somehow, Derek—for she guessed it must be him—had discovered where she'd gone.

"Thank heavens," she said softly.

"Unfortunately, the rescue party is planning to dock immediately."

She glanced at the colonel. "Why is that unfortunate?"

"Because the *Valiant* is close to initiating the Y-drive blast sequence for Halgrek. Military policy doesn't allow any ships within a wide radius of any transport engaging the drive, as the blowback can be deadly. I'm afraid they'll be grounded here for the three months it takes to reach Halgrek."

She glanced at the pitted metal walls, and shivered. "Can't you simply wait until we're gone, and fire the drive then?"

"No—the sequence is hard-coded into the system. It can't be altered, not even by myself, in case of mutiny or prisoner uprising. No matter what, this ship is bound for the prison world." He glanced at the readout above the control panel. "In fifteen minutes."

"Can't the other ship pick me up and then take off again before the Y-Drive engages?" she asked, mind scrambling for alternatives.

He shook his head. "The *Vesper* is fast, but even the quickest craft won't be able to outrun our wake. The turbulence will send you spinning—probably right into Jupiter."

"Might I have something to work calculations on?" she asked, her pulse racing. There had to be another solution besides being trapped aboard the *Valiant* or crushed by

Jupiter's atmosphere. "Also, might I speak to one of your navigational engineers?"

"Johnson there is a navvie." The colonel gestured toward a dark-haired woman further down the control room. "I'll introduce you."

He did so, and also procured pencil and paper for her, handing them over with a bemused expression, but she did not have time to explain. Luckily the navvie knew the answers to most of Diana's questions about the velocity of the *Valiant* and the effect of the Y-Drive.

Even as the outer doors of the hangar opened, admitting a thin silver ship, Diana bent over her equations, calculating. She didn't stop until Colonel Blake interrupted her.

"Your rescue party has arrived," he said.

Diana shoved the paper in her pocket, thanked Johnson for her assistance, and then followed the colonel out of the control room. Her heart hammered in her chest—at the imminent rescue, at the imminent danger. The air in the hangar was cool and smelled of engine fumes.

The colonel ushered her to one side.

"Wait here," he said, as people began to disembark from the small ship.

To her surprise, Director Quinn emerged first, goggles perched on his head. Tipper slipped out next. Catching sight of her, he pelted forward with a glad cry—just as a spray of lightpistol fire pulsed out from the other side of the hanger.

"Tipper, drop!" the a voice called, even as Colonel Blake bellowed for assistance.

"We're under attack!" he yelled. "Protocol seven—stat!"

Tip went down, and Diana's throat closed with fear. She started forward, only to have the colonel grab her arm and yank her out of the line of fire.

"Back in the control room," he said. "Now."

She wanted to argue—but there was little she could do. A corset stay was nothing compared to the deadly blasts of light flying at them. Ducking low, she scurried back toward the safety of the glass-enclosed room.

And then Breggy was there, blocking her way, his teeth bared in a glinting smile.

"I see I've acted just in time," he said, sinking his fingers into her shoulder when she tried to twist away. "How rude of you, to try and run away just as I was taking over the ship."

"You won't succeed," she said. The panic in the back of her mind ratcheted up with every passing second.

"Won't I? It's amazing what the lobsterbacks will do, given sufficient motivation." His gaze slid to the silver ship in the center of the hangar. "Although this is even better. My own escape vehicle. Oh look, there's Officer Byrne."

She wrenched free of Breggy's grip and whirled, to see Derek fighting a group of red-coated soldiers, Nails at his side. Lightpistol fire streaked across the hangar, the short-wave blasts bringing down Colonel Blake's men.

Director Quinn crouched beside his ship, returning the deadly pulses of light, his goggles reflecting the bursts. And Tipper was elbow-crawling toward the renegade guards with the lighpistol, staying close to the wall... She clenched her fingers tight and looked away, trying not to draw attention to him.

"Maybe I ought to bring you with me," Breggy said, reaching for her again. "To provide a bit of amusement."

Part of her wanted to encourage him to take the smaller ship—her too, if he had to—and fly out of the *Valiant*. Directly into the Y-Drive's deadly blast sequence.

But an even bigger part of her wanted to live, to fight, to join her friends at any cost.

She ducked under Breggy's fingers and pulled the corset stay from her boot. Before he could react, she jabbed it at his throat. It penetrated the skin, and his eyes went wide.

"Bastard!" He yanked the metal free.

Damnation—she hadn't hit either his windpipe or his jugular, though a thin trickle of blood crawled down his throat from the puncture wound.

Then she was scrambling away from his fists, trying to find cover while deadly bolts of light pulsed across her vision. He caught her by the hair, and she kicked savagely at him, feeling her metal-toed boots connect with his shins.

It wasn't enough to make him let go, though.

"You'll pay for that," he said, twisting fingers more tightly in her hair.

"Surrender!" Colonel Blake cried.

Diana looked up, to see him standing beside Director Quinn, the director's pistol trained on them. Behind them, Tipper grinned triumphantly, while Nails stayed on the alert, her weapon at the ready. But where was Derek?

Heart clenching, she scanned the bodies on the floor. Not all of them wore uniforms, but of the others—prisoners, she assumed—none were Derek Byrne.

"I don't think so," Breggy called. With his free hand, he

flicked a knife from his sleeve, then brought it to Diana's throat.

She stilled as the cold metal edge met her skin and bit in, just a little. Enough to let her know that Breggy wouldn't hesitate to slit her ear-to-ear the moment her usefulness ran out.

"Put down your guns and clear away from the ship," Breggy continued. "Diver and I are going for a little jaunt."

Expression strained, Director Quinn bent and laid his lightpistol on the floor. The colonel did the same, and slowly they stepped away from the silver form of the Vesper. Tipper made a sound of protest as Nails gave up her weapon, too, then glanced at Diana, his eyes pleading.

No heroics, she silently sent at him, unable to shake her head with the knife lodged at her throat.

In the suddenly quiet hangar, Breggy marched her forward until they reached the ship. At least, when the *Vesper* was destroyed, the gangrunner would be too.

If only she could see Derek one last time.

"Goodbye," Breggy said, his voice gloating.

Tipper's cry of despair rang in Diana's ears as the gangrunner stepped through the hatch, yanking her along with him.

Farewell, she thought. At least it would be a worthwhile death. And fast. The best that any streetrat could hope for.

CHAPTER 26

Derek waited, sweat trickling down his forehead, praying his instincts were correct. His arms and legs shook with the strain of holding himself immobile over the open hatch, but he endured, even as his muscles burned.

Ever since ducking out of the *Vesper* into a firefight, he'd been moving on pure adrenaline: yelling at Tipper to drop, fighting beside Nails, tackling the shooters in the shadows when Tip created a distraction.

And all the while, part of him had known exactly where Diana was. From the moment his feet had hit the decking, his attention had gone to her, like a compass to a magnet.

Horrifyingly, she was, indeed, aboard the *Valiant*.

Thankfully, she seemed unharmed.

And then Breggy had put a blade to her throat, and Derek's brain went white with anger. And pure purpose.

Trusting Nails to fire if given an opening, he'd swung himself back inside the Vesper. He was the last chance, the failsafe if they couldn't get Diana out of Breggy's clutches.

"Steady on," Director Quinn murmured, just loudly

enough for Derek to hear him, as he set his lightpistol down. "Here they come."

Breggy's smug tones sounded just outside the door, and Tipper's cry was the signal for Derek to get ready. He took a deep breath.

The gangrunner backed into the *Vesper*, holding Diana.

Praying the knife wouldn't slip, Derek dropped onto the man's head.

"Agh!" Breggy yelled as they went down. The knife in his hand glinted, blessedly blood-free.

"Get back," Derek said to Diana.

The moment she scrambled free, he used his stunclub on Breggy, at the highest setting. Regretfully, it wouldn't be enough to kill the gangrunner, but his eyes rolled back in his head and his body slumped to the *Vesper's* deck.

"Derek," Diana said. Just his name, but it was everything.

Their gazes met, and everything he could not say he hoped was in his eyes.

Then Tipper was there, arms going about Diana's waist, and the colonel was directing his men to drag Breggy's body back to his cell.

Diana turned to Director Quinn, hovering in the doorway.

"We must leave, immediately," she said. "Or we're stuck on the *Valiant* for months."

"The Y-Drive," he said. "I knew it was a risk, but we had to take it."

"I can't allow you to depart," the colonel said. "We're engaging the jump in..." He glanced up at the chronometer mounted on the *Valiant's* wall. "Six minutes. There's no time to get clear."

"We *have* to get back to Earth," Derek said, pulse hammering in his throat. "There's an imminent threat to the spaceport."

"There is?" Director Quinn gave him a sharp look.

"Yes. A terrorist group is planning to bomb the port next weekend."

"Tell me more—wait, we've no time." The director turned to Colonel Blake. "Can you still get a message back to Earth?"

The colonel shook his head. "All long-range communications have been automatically shut down. They interfere with the Y-Drive's mechanics."

"And once the drive's engaged, there's no hope of contact." Director Quinn's voice was bleak.

"We can get back." Diana pulled a crumpled piece of paper from her pocket. "It's dangerous, of course, but I've run the calculations. There's a good chance we can use the Y-Drive blast to propel us around Jupiter and back on course to Earth—but we need to depart immediately."

"Let's go, then." Director Quinn beckoned to Nails and Tipper. "Everyone, inside. Strap down."

Colonel Blake folded his arms. "I really must protest—"

"I override your concerns," Director Quinn said. "As Director of the Galactic Spaceport of Southampton, I outrank you."

"But do you trust this young lady's calculations?" The colonel shot Diana a troubled glance.

"With my life," Director Quinn said. "Obviously. Come

everyone, quickly now." He settled his goggles more firmly on his head.

"I don't—"

"Open the hatch, commander. Or I'm afraid we might leave a nasty hole in your ship. And tell your control room to make ready for the *Vesper's* immediate liftoff."

Diana glanced at the page of calculations she held in her trembling fingers, then at the countdown clock on the *Valiant's* wall. Five minutes.

"Very well," Colonel Blake said. "You may depart, but for the record, I protest this action." He made the director a stiff bow, then retreated to the glassed-in control room.

"Hurry," Diana said under her breath.

If they delayed much longer, it would be certain death.

But if they stayed aboard the *Valiant*, hundreds of people at the spaceport would die. They had to take the chance.

"Missy Smythe, take navigation." Director Quinn nodded toward the right-hand seat of the cockpit

Feeling ungainly in her skirts, Diana quickly clambered forward and settled in the indicated chair. Behind them, the hatch closed with a quiet clang. Everyone strapped in, and they waited for the hangar bay doors to open.

"Attention, *Vesper*." The colonel's voice crackled through

the comm speaker. "Four minutes until Y-Drive blast. You'll be cleared for takeoff in ten seconds."

The countdown began. Diana looked once more at her paper, covered with scribbled equations, arcs and sines.

"We need to align ourselves along the side of the *Valiant*," she said as the director started the engine. "About midway down the ship, at a forty-degree angle, with Jupiter on our right."

"Starboard, forty-degrees," Director Quinn confirmed.

"And go," the colonel's voice sounded from the comm. "Good luck. You'll need it."

The *Vesper* rose smoothly through the open bay doors, and Diana caught her breath at the sight of the stars blazing outside the cockpit window. She'd never seen anything as beautiful as that clear, cold brilliance. The planets floated, larger spheres of color arranged around the bright orb of the sun. Nearest of all was Jupiter; huge and baleful, watching with one red eye.

Fingers tense, she glanced down at her calculations. She was betting their lives on those figures, and her breath caught at the knowledge. What if she were wrong?

No.

She must trust herself, and Director Quinn's piloting skills, to bring them safely home.

"One and a half minutes until Y-Drive engages," Colonel Blake said over the comm.

It was not enough time.

It was an eternity.

Diana's pulse pounded through her while outside the stars watched, uncaring that five fragile human lives were at stake. Jupiter waited, ready to pull them in and crush them if they veered even the slightest bit off course.

Director Quinn nosed the *Vesper* forward above the larger ship's dark metal exterior, until Diana held up her hand. Matching their speed to the *Valiant*, he began angling the ship's nose out. He was an excellent pilot, and the knowledge helped take the edge off her teeth-gritting anxiety.

"Sixty seconds."

She glanced down at her calculations, triple-checking them once more.

"Ready, back there?" the director called over his shoulder.

"Aye," Tipper called, while Nails murmured her assent.

Diana turned, meeting Derek's gaze. It held nothing but unwavering trust, and that steadied her even more.

"Thirty seconds."

"Full acceleration until we reach apogee," Diana reminded the director.

It was hard to wait, when every nerve was screaming at her they had to go, *now*. But the strange geometry of the Y-Drive's blastoff wake made it far safer for the *Vesper* to ride atop the blast, rather than wait for it to smash them out of space and into Jupiter's waiting arms.

"Then hard to starboard, curving around Jupiter and back home." Director Quinn nodded at her. "We'll be back in my office in time for tea."

She rather desperately hoped so.

The comm crackled to life once more, counting the seconds down. *Five, four, three, two.*

One.

Zero.

Light flared around them. Director Quinn punched the acceleration, his hands steady on the controls. The *Vesper* leaped forward like a startled creature. The entire ship shuddered back and forth and Diana braced herself, white-fingered, against the edge of the control board. Something clanged loose in the cabin, and she heard Derek bite back a curse.

To their right, Jupiter loomed, the strident colors seeming to pulse. White, orange, dark, light. The *Vesper* was moving too slowly, and Diana shot a look at the director.

"Faster," she murmured.

"I can't." His voice was strained.

The secondary blast was going to catch them. If they couldn't get behind Jupiter, the turbulence would throw them right into the gas giant. And once in Jupiter's grasp, there was no escape. She leaned forward and scanned their trajectory. The stars seemed to draw lines in her head, pointing the way.

"Head closer to the planet," she said to the director, her throat tight. "Veer until I tell you to stop."

It was risky, to try and skip like a stone over the outer-most edge of Jupiter's atmosphere, but it was their last chance. Director Quinn nodded and eased the *Vesper* closer to their doom.

"Hold on," Diana called over her shoulder. Her voice sounded shrill in her ears.

The ship bucked, and her stomach rose. She swallowed, hard. Now the *Vesper* was a fish on a tangled line, caught between the pull of Jupiter and the raging turbulence of the Y-Drive's backwash. They could do it though—they had to.

"Ease out," she said, wishing she knew how to fly a ship.

Since she couldn't, she balled her hands into tight fists and fixed all her attention on the view outside the cockpit. A trickle of perspiration slid down the back of her neck.

The stars blurred as they danced on the edge of Jupiter's gravity.

And then, suddenly, the horrible shaking stopped. Diana glanced down, to see the curve of Jupiter floating majestically below them.

On their left, the galaxy shimmered, as though viewed through water. Slowly, the stars quieted as the last of the *Valiant*'s wake flew past.

"Head out two degrees," she whispered, knowing the director would hear her and correct the *Vesper*'s course.

"Done," he said, just as quietly.

One last hiccup rocked the ship as they slipped free of Jupiter's hook. The planet's edge receded, its ghastly colors relegated to nightmares. The *Vesper* was safe, a silver minnow back in the vast waters of space.

"Can we go home now?" Tipper asked plaintively.

"Yes." Director Quinn shot Diana a smile. "Plot a course for earth please, Miss Smythe."

She stared down at the dials and knobs on the navigation panel. "I don't know how."

"Oh, but you do. Look." He lifted a hand, pointing at the blue droplet of Earth hanging in the star-spattered dark.

And with his guidance, hands steady on the controls, she discovered that, indeed, she could take them home.

CHAPTER 28

DEREK HELD TIGHT TO HIS SEAT AS THE *VESPER* SLID INTO ITS private hanger in the Southampton Spaceport. Back on Earth. The relief of it warred with the knowledge of what he must do, whirling like a black hole in his soul. He'd helped save Diana, only to lose her again.

Not to kidnapping or gangrunners, this time. No—she'd go on, living her brilliant, beautiful life, while he sank like a stone beneath icy waters.

He knew that Molly had meant every word about taking him down if he exposed the INR's plot. But he had no other choice.

"Here we are," Director Quinn said, back to his usual jovial self. "Everyone out."

Tipper was first through the hatch, followed by Nails. With stiff fingers, Derek undid the buckles holding him to his chair. Part of him had expected to die, out there in space.

And when he hadn't, during the quiet trip back to Earth he'd wrestled with the choices he'd made. The future he faced because of them, and the bitter consequences he must endure.

At least Diana was safe, and the spaceport would be as well. It was cold comfort, but still, he took it.

Director Quinn gave Derek a pointed look as he ducked out of the *Vesper*, and then it was just the two of them left inside. Derek and Diana.

"Well," she said, coming aft and settling on the chair next to his. "Here we are."

Damnú, she was beautiful. The intelligence in her clear gray eyes, the honey-colored strands of hair loose about her face, her stubborn chin and calm perseverance—everything combined to make her more dear to him than he could say.

And, in fact, he never would. It was one small pain he could spare Diana. No matter how she might feel about him, she did not need to hear him profess his love and then see him consigned to a prison cell. Or worse. With a flash of dark humor, he wondered if he'd have been better off simply staying aboard the *Valiant*.

"Yes," he said, echoing her words. "Here we are."

"How did you find me? When I woke up inside the *Valiant*, I thought I was done for." She caught her breath, a sharp intake of memory.

He wanted to pummel Lord Atkinson bloody for causing her such pain.

"Tipper came to tell me you'd disappeared," he said. "We both knew you wouldn't just leave without a word."

"I promised, don't you remember? Tipper's as dear as family to me now." She shook her head, as if trying to reconcile herself to the fact, then reached and set one of her hands on his. "And Derek, you—"

"We went to the spaceport," he said. "Lord Atkinson was there, and I guessed by his actions that he'd somehow managed to kidnap you and put you aboard the *Valiant*. Luckily for all of us, I was right."

The feel of her hand on his, warm and secure, made his throat ache. His heart was scorching in his chest, and he could not bear to hear her say she cared for him. She'd lost enough, already.

"I owe you my life," she said, leaning forward.

Too close. The clean smell of her skin made his heart race, and all he wanted to do was kiss her. Which was a disastrous idea.

"And we owe Director Quinn, too." Derek awkwardly rose and sidled around her chair. "We should go thank him, together."

"Oh." Disappointment shadowed her expression. "But after that, perhaps we—"

"I also need to tell the director and Nails about the plot to bomb the spaceport."

And after that, you'll despise me.

He'd been lying all along, and he didn't think she could forgive him for that. He couldn't forgive himself for the way the INR had used him, either. What a blind, bloody fool he'd been.

Derek disembarked from the *Vesper*, but couldn't help waiting for her, offering his hand in assistance as she stepped out of the hatch. Just one more touch. One more memory to take away with him to whatever dark place he was bound.

They joined the others at the lift. When they arrived at the top floor, Director Quinn ushered them into the conference room and sent his secretary for tea.

"Sit down," he said, gesturing.

They settled around the table: Tipper and Nails, Director Quinn. And Diana. Derek was the last to take his seat.

"First off," the director said, "I must congratulate each and every one of you for that extraordinary rescue mission."

"Don't forget yourself," Tipper piped up. "We'd still be stuck on Earth if it wasn't for you and the *Vesper*."

"We all played our part," Director Quinn said. "And now, Derek, please tell us about this plot against the spaceport that you discovered."

Nails gave a sharp nod. "Good police work there, I'd say."

The irony stung the back of Derek's throat.

"Not so much. You see, I know about the plot because…" He swallowed, hard. "Because I'm the one that provided the information to the terrorists to begin with."

"What?" Nails half rose, one hand going to her stun cuff.

Good instincts there, but then, he already knew he trusted her implicitly in a fight.

"Explain," Director Quinn said.

Derek squeezed his eyes shut a moment, and then opened them. He fixed his gaze on the director's face, as he couldn't bear to look at Diana.

"I've been working for the INR all along," he said. "I

joined the Southampton Police in order to infiltrate the spaceport and gather information."

Each word was a heavy stone dropped into his body, until he could scarcely take the weight. There was no use trying to explain what he thought the INR was going to do with the knowledge. The fact of the matter was, he'd broken the law in any number of ways.

Nails narrowed her eyes at him. "Are you certain?"

That prompted a bitter bark of laughter. "Aye. I knew what I was doing."

"How could you?" Tipper asked, his voice wobbling.

"I was a fool." Finally, Derek forced himself to meet Diana's gaze. "I'm sorry."

She watched him calmly, but he could see the deep hurt in her eyes.

"Were you simply using me all along, then?" she asked.

"No." Further excuses dried in his throat. "Arrest me. I'll gladly tell you everything I know about the others involved."

"Molly," Diana said.

"Yes." He wasn't surprised that her quick mind was already seeing the patterns.

"I have to take you into custody," Nails said. She didn't look happy about it.

"But Derek saved Di!" Tipper turned to Nails, his eyes wide. "He can't just go to prison."

"The entire thing is incredibly complicated." Director Quinn pinched the bridge of his nose, his expression more troubled than Derek had ever seen. "Please, give us everything you can about the INR's plans. It's of paramount importance to stop this attack."

"Of course." Derek rose and held out his arm for the stun cuff.

Nails got to her feet, frowning at him. "I trust you to come quietly."

Head bowed, he followed her to the door.

"Sir?" The director's secretary peered around Nails where she stood blocking the threshold. "You have a visitor —a Viscount Smythe. May I show him in?"

"Is he related to our Miss Smythe?" the director asked.

"He claims to be, sir."

"Might be a trap," Nails said. She glanced at Derek. "Sit back down. I'll formally arrest you, after we hear what this fellow has to say."

CHAPTER 29

Diana sank back in her chair, her mind whirling. Her heart breaking.

How could Derek have lied to her, to all of them? She reviewed every interaction she'd had with him, trying to understand. Grasping for any bit of truth, hoping to see the glint of it shining up through the muck of their past.

She drew in a deep breath, trying to regain her equilibrium so that she could think clearly again. Surely the equations would line up. Surely she could make sense of this, somehow.

Just as she caught her balance, Le ushered an older gentleman into the conference room, and her world tilted again.

Father? The word trembled through her.

No, it could not be. Her father was dead—and yet, this man looked so familiar, with his gray-streaked hair and jutting nose.

"May I present Viscount Smythe," Le said. "He claims to be related to Miss Smythe."

"Diana?" The viscount halted, fixing her with his gray eyes.

The cogs in her mind spun, spun, then clicked together. She knew this man… he was…

"Uncle Xavier?" Her voice wobbled on the name.

"Dear heavens!" he said. "It *is* you!"

He strode forward, arms open, and, without thinking, she jumped up to embrace him. He smelled of expensive tobacco and oranges. When she finally pulled back, both their eyes were wet with tears.

"How did you find me?" she asked.

She'd been lost and found twice in less than a day, and she felt as though she might shatter from it. Like a piece of metal stressed beyond bearing, or a stone with a hidden, fatal crack running through the center.

"I saw the notice," Uncle Xavier said. "I couldn't be sure it was you, Diana, though you look so very much like your mother. I had to discover more, and this office was listed as the contact for further information."

"The notice?" Director Quinn asked.

Le made him a slight bow. "In the off chance that Miss Smythe was not, in fact, aboard the *Valiant*, I took the liberty of issuing a missing persons holo. It was broadcast widely."

"Indeed." The director nodded at his secretary. "A good though. And I suppose it worked out for the best, if Miss Smythe is now reunited with her family."

"What became of you?" Uncle Xavier took her by the shoulders and scanned her face. "You were reported dead. There was a body, I attended the funeral of your whole family. And then I left Earth for several years."

Diana shook her head. "I don't know. During the accident, I was thrown free of the carriage, and woke up in an orphanage. I couldn't remember anything for quite some time, and when I finally did, they didn't believe me."

She bit her lip, remembering the harsh laughter of the matron when Diana insisted she lived in a mansion in Mayfair. To prove the woman wrong, Diana had snuck out of the orphanage and made her way home.

But it was not her home any longer. The unfamiliar butler at the door had turned her away, saying a different family lived there now, and they didn't condone beggars.

Bewildered, she'd gone around to the kitchens, only to find all new servants there. The cook had given her a few scraps and sent her on her way. There had been no one to turn to, no one who would recognize her, or accept her story as true.

Uncle Xavier frowned, carving deep grooves on either side of his mouth. "There were a number of orphans on the omnibus when it crashed. I suppose you might have been taken for one of them. Still, what a monumental travesty! I can't begin to tell you how sorry I am for all you've been through."

That was hardly the worst of it. The ache of losing her family was a dim echo compared with the sharp, immediate pain of losing Derek. She glanced at him, memories crowding her mind of all the times they'd shared together.

I thought I loved you.

He regarded her silently, his blue eyes shadowed.

"What will you do now?" Tipper asked. "Does that mean you're a toff, Di?"

Uncle Xavier's expression eased. "If the young man

means to ask about your social status, then yes, you are a young lady of the nobility. Your great-aunt is the Duchess of Penderly, after all. I'm sure she'd be delighted to take you in, as she's lost so much of her family."

"I… don't know what to say." Truly, Diana felt as though she stood on the edge of a precipice, winds whirling all about her, threatening to push her off into the cloud-filled void.

Would she fall, or would she fly? Her ability to sense the trajectory of her own choices had failed her, leaving her shaken and completely unsure.

"No need to decide just now," her uncle said. "I know this must come as a bit of a shock to you."

It was the gravest understatement. Diana felt as though her world would never turn perfectly on any axis, ever again.

Director Quinn looked at her. "I would like to remind you that you still have a position here at the spaceport, Diana. If you'd like to remain."

"I don't know." Everything crowded in on her, the lines of chance and opportunity hopelessly tangled until she just wanted to find a dark corner, curl up into a ball, and weep.

Seeing the look on her face, Tipper jumped up and wrapped his arms about her shoulders.

"Don't worry," he whispered. "It will all come out right."

"Well then." Nails stepped forward. "As long as there's no danger to Miss Smythe, I'll be taking Officer Byrne away."

No.

Diana trapped the word behind her teeth.

Slowly, Derek rose from his chair. He paused beside

her, and she was torn between pummeling him for his betrayal, or giving him a soft, single kiss goodbye. Instead, she did neither, just stood there, trying not to give in to the sobs gathering in her throat.

"I wish you the happiest life imaginable," Derek said, meeting her gaze. "You deserve nothing but the best. Goodbye, Diana."

She gave him a tight nod. If she spoke, she would cry, and if she began to cry, she wasn't sure she'd ever be able to stop. Only Tipper's arms, still tight about her shoulders, kept her from falling to pieces right there on Director Quinn's plush carpet.

Spine straight, Derek turned away and let Nails lead him out of the conference room.

He did not look back.

CHAPTER 30

DIANA SHOT A GLANCE AT THE STATELY OLD WOMAN AT HER side as they preceded toward the crowded ballroom of yet another high-society soiree. Her great-aunt was garbed in an elegant emerald-green gown, with matching jewels at her neck, wrists, fingers, hair… With a sigh, Diana stopped herself from counting up the wealth of gems adorning the Duchess of Penderly.

Her own jewels were paltry in comparison, and she liked it that way. A small set of rubies at her throat and a single ring were quite sufficient, no matter how much her great-aunt might disapprove.

"Diana, you are a young lady of Quality now," the duchess had said with a stern look. "It would behoove you to comport yourself accordingly."

"I'm comfortable as I am," she'd replied.

She was trying, truly, but it was difficult. Ever since arriving in London with Uncle Xavier a fortnight ago, she'd done her best to behave within the strict confines of proper society. But by all the stars, the nobs could be tiresome.

Of course, she was also desperately trying to distract herself from the might-have-beens that still fogged her thoughts. It had been too difficult, trying to return to her work at the spaceport. The cloudiness of her mind made it so that she could scarcely see the trajectories that had once been drawn, clear as lines of light, in the air before her.

"Don't fret yourself over it," Director Quinn had told her, his voice warm. "You've had a calamitous week. Take some time off, accept your uncle's offer to go up to London. Perhaps that will help."

Neither of them had mentioned Derek. He remained in jail, though the plot to bomb the spaceport had been foiled and key members of the INR rounded up. By removing herself from Southampton, Diana had also removed the temptation to visit him. Seeing him again would only wound them both.

The trial to determine his fate was fast approaching, though, and despite herself, her heart ticked down the days.

Unfortunately, pretending to be part of Society was not proving to be a sufficient distraction.

Balls and parties, teas and musicales... Compared to scrounging up a living as a streetrat, the lavish lifestyle of the Duchess of Penderly and her friends was nearly incomprehensible. When Diana had said as much to Uncle Xavier on one of his visits, he'd given her a curious look.

"Don't you remember growing up in the nobility?" he'd asked. "I'd thought this would all be familiar to you. Like a fish returning to water, yes?"

It wasn't though. Occasionally she'd have a dim, echoing sense of recognition, but mostly she felt as though she were trying to wear garments three sizes too small. The clothing of her childhood, which she had long since outgrown.

"Remember," her great-aunt said as they reached the ballroom, "No dancing with the same partner more than twice in an evening. Once is preferable. You don't want to play favorites, after all. At least, not yet."

Diana let out a silent sigh. "Yes, Aunt."

She'd tried to call the duchess "Your Grace," as was customary for that title, but her great-aunt would have none of that. "Milady" was too subservient, and "great-aunt" too much of a mouthful. The question of the duchess's given name was never raised, though Diana thought it might be Hortense.

So "Aunt" it was, despite the fact that three generations separated them.

"Her Grace, the Duchess of Penderly, and Lady Diana Smythe," the butler announced as they stepped over the threshold into the brightly lit ballroom.

Unlike the People's Cotillion Diana had gone to, the balls the duchess frequented in London were only attended by the highest orders of the nobility. Snobbery was as thick in the air as expensive perfume, and any social misstep Diana might make was duly noted and gossiped over.

That hadn't seemed to keep a fair number of eligible men from paying attention to Diana, however; much to her great-aunt's dry approval.

"You're a catch," the duchess said. "Despite your past, you've an excellent pedigree, not to mention being an heiress. Be sure to show some discernment about whom you will allow to court you."

No one knew about her sordid past, of course. Uncle Xavier and the duchess had put about some vague story of Diana being sent to live with distant relatives after her family was killed in the carriage accident. They pretended that she'd only just come to London to be presented to Society.

And to find a proper spouse, which seemed to be the chief occupation of all the other young ladies she'd met so far, not to mention a goodly portion of the gentlemen.

"I'm not certain I want *any* of them to court me," she replied.

From their vantage point at the edge of the room, Diana could pick out a number of fellows who had sought her out at the half-dozen social events the duchess had insisted she attend.

Unfortunately, they noted her presence as well, and quickly converged.

The sandy-haired gentleman whose eyes glazed over whenever Diana began to speak. The foppishly dressed lord who laughed too much. The arrogant baronet who reminded her rather too strongly of Lord Atkinson.

At least her kidnapper had been deported off planet. Sadly, not to a prison world, but instead to a "sanitarium planet" where convicted nobility were incarcerated for the rest of their lives. She hoped Lord Atkinson reaped all the rewards of his odious behavior.

The evidence of wealth was all around her, the men courtly to the point of foolishness, their manners polished even more brightly than their shoes, but it only served to make her feel out of place. She might look the part of a well-bred young lady, but under the silks and jewels, the layers of nano-lifted skirts and artfully arrayed hair, a part of her was still Diver, the streetrat.

And she didn't mind—but she knew that the possible future husbands signing their names to her dance card would.

This was not the life she wanted. Pretending to be something she wasn't, denying her past in the slums and the spaceport. As one of her would-be suitors whirled her precisely about the dance floor, the knowledge coalesced into a clear, hard conviction.

It was all she could do to endure the last waltz. Her partner was dark haired and blue eyed and made her think of Derek—not that painful thoughts of him were ever far from her mind. With a pang, she recalled the first waltz she'd ever danced, Derek holding her lightly in his arms as they twirled about the room, laughing together at their stumbles.

There was no laughter here, except the bright, forced kind. And stumbles of any sort were greatly frowned upon.

At the end of the dance, she managed a graceful enough curtsey, then fled back to her great-aunt.

"I'm ready to leave," Diana said.

"Hmph." The duchess peered at her, but seemed disinclined to argue. Perhaps she was also realizing that this experiment was at an end.

In the velvet-upholstered carriage, Diana laced her gloved fingers in her lap and gathered her courage.

"I'm sorry, Aunt," she said, "but can't stay in London any longer. I thank you, so very much, for taking me into your home and giving me all this..." She gestured to her gown and jewels, the coach, the bright gaslamps of Mayfair passing outside the windows.

"But it is not the life for you." The duchess let out a weary sigh, her years suddenly showing more clearly upon her face. "I understand. I'd hoped that you could step into Society and take your place here, but clearly it's not to be."

Diana couldn't tell if her great-aunt was being realistic or was, in fact, deeply disappointed. The old woman had spent decades keeping any trace of untoward emotion from her expression, and an acquaintance of only two weeks wasn't long enough for Diana to decipher the look in her eyes.

"I am sorry." Diana was, truly.

It had been a lovely little wisp of a dream while it lasted. But it had been the dream of a naïve young girl who knew nothing of the world except a sheltered corner of London Society.

The mist in her mind cleared further, and she drew in a deep breath of the night air.

"What will you do?" her great-aunt asked.

"I rather think... I'd like to become a star pilot." The words surprised her, but even as Diana spoke them, she knew they were right.

"A star pilot. Well. How unusual."

"There are women pilots," Diana replied, a little hotly. Not a great number, of course, but some. "If you want to withdraw my inheritance—"

"Oh goodness, no." The duchess waved her hand back and forth, as though swatting away an annoying insect. "You are still a Smythe, and entitled to a portion of the family fortune. It's not as though there are that many others left to give it to. Xavier is terribly spoiled already, and has too much money of his own as it is. I'm sure you'll put it to good use."

"I will." Diana knew that much, though the details were hazy.

A way to take streetrats to the stars. A school. She was beginning to see the possibilities, like constellations glimpsed through a scrim of night clouds. Before long, she trusted the wind would sweep the air clear and the patterns would, once again, burn brightly in her mind.

CHAPTER 31

"Di!" Tipper barreled into her as she stepped through the doorway of Number 54 Queensway Tower. "You came back!"

"I did." She ruffled his hair, noting it was overdue for a wash, and smiled fondly at him. Some things never changed.

"You were away forever," he said. "I thought I was doomed for a bachelor."

"I was hardly gone more than a fortnight! And besides, you were invited to live with the duchess, too. Not my fault you turned down her hospitality."

Tipper made a face. "London's for nobs and flash folk. Southamptonport's the place for me."

The truth was, the boy had taken one look at the Duchess of Penderly's grand town house, full of shiny knickknacks and rigid expectations, and demanded that Uncle Xavier take him right back to Southampton. He'd seen right away what it had taken Diana two weeks to discover—but then, Tip had always been a clever one.

"You've the right of it," Diana said. "But I'm home now."

"Just in time, too." He hefted her valise and started hauling it back to her bedroom.

She paused in the kitchen and took an appreciative sniff. "Just in time for fresh scones?"

"Aye, that too." He set her luggage down and bounded back to the kitchen. "But Derek's hearing is tomorrow! It got moved up in the docket. I sent you a message."

Thank heavens she'd decided to return sooner rather than later.

"We must have crossed paths outside of London." She began unbuttoning her pelisse, trying to ignore the fact that her fingers were trembling. "How's it looking for him?"

"Well enough. I don't think he's going for transportation, at any rate. Not after he fingered the INR lot. Special dispensation for cooperating with the law or suchlike."

The tightness in her chest eased somewhat.

"That's good news. Now, how about you butter me a scone while I go wash up?"

As she dried her face on a soft towel, Diana wondered why she hadn't been called up as a witness. Derek had saved her life, after all. Wasn't that worth something? Or had everyone assumed she'd gone off to live the grand life of a lady, and didn't care one whit any more.

The fact of it was, she did care. A great deal.

Now that she was back, the Tipper-shaped hole in her heart was mended. Next to the question of Derek, missing Tip had been an ache she'd also tried to ignore as she'd attempted to fit herself back into the life of the nobility.

It had been a worthwhile, if failed, experiment,

however. She'd come to that realization during the return trip to Southampton. If she'd never gone to London, a part of her would always have wondered if she belonged in the world of the gentry.

That question was now laid to rest. Diana Smythe's future held far more than a proper, stuffy existence wedded to a proper, stuffy gentleman.

As for the Derek-shaped hole in her heart? Well, she would attend his trial tomorrow, and discover an answer to that question, too. Until then, she could only look to the stars, and hope.

DEREK COMBED HIS HAIR AND THEN ATTEMPTED A BETTER knot on his neckcloth, without much success. The pitted metal mirror in his cell wasn't helpful in either endeavor, but at least they'd given him a comb, and a tie, and brought his father's old suit for him to wear.

He'd be presentable for the hearing, if not the very picture of fashion. Although, Lord Atkinson had proved that looking like a fine gentleman was no true reflection of character.

"Ready?" Nails asked from the other side of the bars.

Not at all, but he had no choice. At least this was a hearing before a judge, and not a full public trial.

That said, as Nails and another guard led him into the wood-paneled room in the Southampton Judiciary Building, he found that a small crowd had gathered on the benches. Director Quinn was there, and Tipper, and...

Derek nearly missed a step when he saw Diana. She was

dressed in a dove gray coat and skirts, her hair pinned up in a bun that was already unraveling a little at the edges.

Their eyes met, and he couldn't breathe. What was she doing in Southampton? She was a lady now, swept into the heart of Society, her every need met. She should be off at some picnic with dukes and princes and the like, not sitting in a windowless room of the court waiting to hear the fate of one unfortunate constable.

Once, for a brief, bright moment, their lives had intersected as equals. Not as police officer and streetrat, not as convict and lady, but as Officer Byrne and Miss Smythe. There had been a chance for them, then—except for the paths he'd already taken.

He dropped his gaze to the dark floorboards and walked past. Nails escorted him to a chair in the front row before the judge's bench and he numbly sat on the hard wood. The air was stale in his lungs. He quashed the little sparks of hope that tried to flare through him.

The barrister that Director Quinn had hired for Derek had been optimistic about the outcome. More optimistic than Derek himself, who'd braced himself for the worst. He couldn't imagine much of a life beyond this point, no matter what happened.

His career was over. Diana was lost to him twice over—by his own lies, and by the fact that she was gentry now. Their worlds were too far apart to ever meet again.

He snuck another glance in her direction, then quickly looked away when he saw she was watching him.

A thick folder tucked under one arm, Derek's barrister, a steady fellow named Mr. Whortley, strode into the room, accompanied by the opposing counsel. The two men seemed amiable enough, which he supposed was a good sign.

The first order of business would be the damning evidence of Derek's collusion in the plot to bomb the Southampton Spaceport. He'd given the police every shred of information he had about the local members of the INR. Apparently they'd put it to good use. Nails told him the officials had been able to track down and arrest one of the national leaders who'd been closely involved in the conspiracy.

"The leader will be giving testimony at the hearing," Derek's barrister had warned him. "It won't look good, of course. They'll try to bring you down along with them, but I won't let that happen."

Derek had only nodded. He couldn't afford to believe anything but the worst.

There was a slight stir at the door as the guards brought in the INR leader, and whispers rustled through the crowd. Derek turned his head, and was shocked to see Molly O'Rourke being escorted down the aisle.

Her red hair looked very bright against her drab prison dress. When her gaze met Derek's she gave him a narrow-eyed look, hatred sparking in her eyes.

The guards settled her in the front row beyond Derek, then took their places to either side. Molly leaned past the guard seated between them, and fixed Derek with a hard look.

"Traitor," she said in a low voice. "You betrayed the cause of all Ireland."

"You might think so," Mr. Whortley said from his place

at Derek's right, his tone calm. "And yet, my client served a higher cause."

"Imperialism? Ha! There's no worse cause than that."

The barrister gave her a steely look. "I was speaking, ma'am, of Life. The explosion your group was plotting would have killed dozens, disabled far more, and stranded thousands of travelers throughout the galaxy, as well as causing supply shortages and untold distress. Mr. Byrne did humanity a fine service when he confessed everything to the authorities."

She blew a sharp breath out of her nose and folded her arms, but said nothing more.

The judge called the room to order. He swore the witnesses to speak the truth, and then the hearing began. Molly went first, describing in excruciating detail how Derek had been involved with the INR in Dublin and had pledged to serve the cause of the resistance.

At this, Mr. Whortley stood, and the judge granted him permission to question Molly. The barrister turned to her, his expression smooth.

"You say that my client, Mr. Byrne, was a member of the terrorist group calling themselves the Irish Nationalist Resistance?" he asked.

"Yes." Molly's face was hard. "He owed a debt to us, and vowed to repay it, even with his very life, if called upon."

"And he was made fully aware of those acts, as a full-fledged member of your organization?"

"Aye. I've told you that already."

"Please roll up your left sleeve, Miss O'Rourke. To the shoulder, yes. Thank you." Mr. Whortley gestured at the mark tattooed on the pale skin of Molly's upper arm. "Mr. Byrne, do you know what this tattoo represents?"

"I don't," Derek said, his gut beginning to clench with suspicion.

"Have you seen such a mark before?" the barrister asked.

"Yes." Derek glanced again at the triangle crossed with three lines. "There was a tattoo like that on a dead body the Southampton Police fished out of the river."

"But do you know what it signifies?"

"I've only heard rumors," Derek said. "Nothing substantive about what that mark means. Frankly, I'd like to know. The case hasn't yet been solved."

Mr. Whortley gave a short nod, then turned back to Molly. "Would you care to enlighten the court as to the nature of your tattoo?"

"I would not." Her voice was tight.

"Very well. Then I shall." He turned to the white-wigged judge presiding from his high bench. "Your honor, I have here sworn testimony from another member of the INR that this mark is given to fully-indoctrinated members as an initiation rite when they make their final pledges of loyalty. The man cannot testify publically, for fear of his life. I'm certain you understand. He's currently under the protection of Scotland Yard, but I can arrange a private meeting, if you'd like."

Mr. Whortley placed his folder on the judge's desk.

The judge glanced at the other barrister. "Sir, do you have any objection?"

"No, your honor. I've reviewed the contents, and there is nothing there I can take issue with."

"Bastard," Molly said in a low voice. Her barrister ignored her.

"A moment." The judge opened the folder and paged through the contents, nodding thoughtfully.

For the first time, Derek felt his hopes rise.

After several moment, the judge closed the folder and nodded to Mr. Whortley.

"Carry on," he said.

"Thank you, your honor." The barrister turned and beckoned to one of the male guards.

Derek recognized the fellow; he'd stood watch the few times Derek had been allowed to bathe. It hadn't been comfortable being under the man's scrutiny, but it had been worth it to wash off the filth of the jail.

Too bad it accumulated again so quickly.

After confirming that the guard recognized Derek, and had, most embarrassingly, seen him naked, Mr. Whortly got to the meat of his questioning.

"To the best of your knowledge, does Mr. Byrne possess any tattoos?" the barrister asked.

"Not as I ever saw." The guard grinned. "And I saw 'bout every bit of him. Nice enough looking, if you like them solid. Got all his parts, and they're—"

"That's quite sufficient," Mr. Whortley said, cutting the fellow off.

Derek felt his neck flush. By all the stars and comets, did the man have to be so blunt? He stared at the grained wood paneling and tried to ignore the fact that Diana, of all people, was in the room.

The guard was allowed to return to his seat, and Mr. Whortley turned once more to Molly.

"Although you claim that Mr. Byrne was acting as a full member of the INR, it would appear that he was not, in fact, indoctrinated into your organization. He does not bear the tattoo identifying him as such, and he did not even recognize what it meant."

"He was working for us, right enough," Molly said, her voice bitter. "His job was to infiltrate the spaceport, though we had to help that along, too."

"In what way?" Mr. Whortley's expression stayed mild, but Derek saw his fingers flex with interest.

"Officer Byrne there is a mite slow," Molly said. "So we threw him a bit of bait. A mystery to solve that would lead him into the spaceport."

"The galactic smuggler's ring on the corpse," Derek said.

All the pieces were clicking into place. The murder hadn't been tied to the spaceport at all—but it was meant to look that way.

Indeed, in all probability the body hadn't been the result of a murder at all, but a casualty of one of the INR's recent actions. Fortunately, whoever had set it up had overlooked one small, crucial detail: the INR tattoo.

"You needed to get into the port," Molly said. "But if we'd told you what was afoot, you'd have bungled it. As you did anyway." Her expression darkened. "I didn't know the body was one of ours. That was stupidity, and when I find out who's responsible—"

"You won't be in a position to do much about it," Mr. Whortley said. "As I understand the events, your organization provided a victim. The resulting investigation was supposed to give my client an innocent reason to work with Spaceport Security and gain access to the spaceport's inner workings, thus paving the way for your act of espionage. Correct?"

Molly pressed her lips together and didn't answer.

"Miss O'Rourke." Her barrister came to stand before her, scowling. "You've done yourself a great disservice by withholding a number of facts from me."

"And would they have helped at all?" She stared at him, and he was the first to look away.

"Anyhow," he said. "Are you finished with my client, Mr. Whortley?"

"I am." Derek's barrister turned to the judge. "Your honor, I would like to call Mr. Derek Byrne to the stand."

CHAPTER 32

DEREK'S BREATH RASPED IN HIS THROAT, SEEMING LOUD IN the expectant silence that had fallen over the room.

Bones aching like an old man, he rose and went to the witness's chair. From this vantage point, he could see everyone clearly. Tipper, perching like an anxious bird on the edge of the bench. Nails, her face stoic as a statue. Director Quinn, brows furrowed yet still with a twinkle in his eye.

And Diana, fingers laced tightly together, her expression a blend of hope and worry.

For him? The thought gave him heart.

"Mr. Byrne," his barrister said, his hands folded at his back, "please share with the court what kind of information the INR asked you to procure, and what purpose you believed it would serve."

"They asked for shipping schedules," Derek answered. "It was my understanding the INR was seeking to smuggle people off Earth. Fugitives, escaped prisoners, enemies of the British Empire, and the like. They also wanted information about spaceport security. For the same purpose, I thought—to help them slip people into the port and then onto ships bound out from Earth."

Mr. Whortley gave him an encouraging nod. "And when you found out that the INR was planning to bomb the spaceport, instead, what did you do?"

"Traitor," Molly whispered, a furious note in her voice.

Derek ignored her as best he could. "I informed the Director of the Spaceport and one of his top security guards that there was a threat."

Mr. Whortley pursed his lips. "Even knowing that you would be incriminated when the connection between yourself and the INR was revealed?"

"Yes," Derek said. "I'd rather save more lives than just my own."

A melancholy smile touched Diana's lips, and was gone. *Damnú*, he didn't want her thinking him a hero. He'd made his bed with the INR right enough.

"Speaking of saving lives," Mr. Whortley said, "I understand you were a key member of the team that rescued Lady Diana Smythe from the *Valiant*. Kindly describe those events."

Derek did, starting with the kidnapping, his hunch that Lord Atkinson had put Diana aboard the prison transport, and the events that had transpired once they'd reached the *Valiant*. He tried to keep it as dry and factual as possible, though he didn't know how well he succeeded.

When he finished, he felt as emptied of energy as a depleted stunclub.

The opposing counsel declined to question him, much

to Molly's contempt, and Derek was allowed to leave the stand.

"Any more witnesses?" the judge asked.

"No, your honor," Mr. Whortley said

The other barrister simply shook his head.

"Then if you will all give me a moment," the judge said to the room in general, "I will ponder the facts of the case. You may speak quietly amongst yourselves."

Murmurs of conversation sprung up, and Mr. Whortley turned to Derek.

"It's going well," he said encouragingly. "The fact that the judge is just looking over his notes means he's mostly decided which way the court will rule, which I'm thinking is good news for us."

"If you say so." Exhaustion weighed upon Derek, and he wished for it all to be over. Wished for Diana to be gone from there, so she wouldn't have to see him led in stun cuffs from the room, bound for transportation.

After what felt like an eternity, the judge gave two sharp raps with his gavel.

"Silence, please," he said.

Derek's exhaustion fled, replaced by jagged expectation.

Thud, thud, went his pulse as he waited for the judge to speak. Despite Mr. Whortley's nimble handling of the question of Derek's INR involvement, he was certain he faced a sentence of life transportation. If not worse.

When the room settled, the judge leaned forward, sweeping the front row with his gaze. "Upon consideration of the evidence, I have reached my decision concerning Mr. Byrne's fate."

The silence deepened even further, an endless pit, waiting for Derek to fall, and fall…

"Mr. Byrne," the judge said, "you have acted against the interests of the Crown, colluded with a known terrorist group, and passed them confidential information. These are serious offenses."

Derek nodded.

"Your involvement with the INR cannot be condoned," the judge continued. "Despite the fact that you came to the authorities when you realized they planned to set off a bomb inside the spaceport, association with a known terrorist group is unforgiveable. The whys and wherefores of how you fell in with them is of little consequence."

The audience stirred, and Derek heard someone let out a quiet gasp. The judge lifted his head and scanned the crowd. He paused when he saw Director Quinn, then turned his attention back to Derek.

"On the other hand," he said, "your quick thinking and keen instincts helped rescue a valued member of our society. While one life saved does not right the balance against the lives that would have ended had you not come to the authorities, it is a variable worth considering. In addition, you put your own life in the balance, several times."

The precipice receded a little, though Derek's pulse still hammered relentlessly through his veins.

Helping rescue Diana was perhaps the single best thing he'd ever done in his life, and he was glad the court recognized it. Confessing to his involvement with the INR had been easy, in comparison.

I don't believe one's past controls one's future. He heard the words as clearly as if Diana were standing beside him, whispering them into his ear.

"Quiet." The judge rapped his gavel once upon his desk, silencing the buzz of speculation rising in the room. Derek braced himself for the verdict. Beside him, Mr. Whortley set a hand on his shoulder.

"In light of all the evidence," the judge continued, "it is the decision of this court that Mr. Byrne serve out a sentence of banishment for life from this, our home planet. We consider it a sufficient punishment. This hearing is now concluded."

The room erupted, Tipper's cheering rising over the noise. The judge rose and retired into his chambers, black robes billowing.

"A fine outcome." Mr. Whortley stood and clapped Derek on the shoulder. "I couldn't have hoped for better."

Derek rose, feeling stunned. He'd numbed his senses so thoroughly over the past weeks of imprisonment, bracing himself for the worst, that he wasn't sure how to take the news.

"How long, before I have to leave Earth?" he asked.

"In matters like this, usually you'll have a month or two to set your affairs in order, bid family farewell, and the like." The barrister gave him a keen-eyed look. "Not to mention deciding where you want to go."

Exile. Not transportation, or imprisonment. Derek's life was his own again. The knowledge swelled within him, as though he'd swallowed a seed that had suddenly grown all out of proportion.

Where *would* he go? He hadn't the faintest idea. Somewhere beyond the INR's reach, that much was certain. It shouldn't prove too difficult, as the terrorist organization was focused on reclaiming Ireland's independence on its home soil, not dispersing out to the stars.

He did know he'd go home and say goodbye to his mother, pay his respects at Seamus's and his father's graves. Smell the fresh damp of the rain on the Dublin cobbles and raise a pint in the old neighborhood pub.

And do his utmost to stop thinking about Diana Smythe. He knew she'd never forgive him for his lies.

Unfortunately, the young woman in question was coming toward him, accompanied by Tipper, Nails, and Director Quinn.

"Splendid news!" The director reached Derek and took his hand, pumping it vigorously. "Well, not the part about being banished from Earth, of course. But it could have been far, far worse."

"Aye," Derek said.

"I'm sorry you have to go." Tipper looked up at him. There was a smudge next to his nose—flour maybe, or baking powder. "But just think—you could go anywhere you wanted!"

"I could." The problem being that Derek had no notion of where that might be.

Then Diana was there, standing before him, and all his yearning for what might have been was a fist in his gut.

"Miss Smythe," he managed to say. "You're looking well."

She opened her mouth, then closed it again, as if reconsidering her words.

"Hello, Derek," she finally said. "Do you think, before you go, that you might be free for dinner?"

"No." He could not, could *not*, go down that path.

His battered heart would not survive the strain of trying to regain her friendship, only to lose it again when he left the planet forever.

Her expression fell, and he was sorry for the shadows on her face. But he still would not change his mind. Lady Diana Smythe was not for him, and never would be. She deserved a better destiny than anything a nearly-criminal exile from Earth could offer.

"I imagine you'll be busy making ready to depart," Director Quinn said, in an obvious attempt to smooth over the awkwardness of the moment. "Perhaps we could all dine together at some point, before you go."

Derek gave him a stiff nod. "I'll let you know. And thank you, director, for your help in this matter. Mr. Whortley was an excellent barrister."

"After what you did to save Miss Smythe, I could hardly abandon you to the mercies of a public defender," Director Quinn said. "I'm glad everything turned out as well as it did."

"Me too," Tipper said.

Nails, standing behind him, simply nodded.

Derek hardened his heart, then glanced at Diana. He must make it clear they had no future together—for both their sakes.

"Thank you for coming down from London," he said. "But you needn't trouble yourself any further on my account."

She rocked back, blinking, clearly hurt by his words.

It's better this way, Derek thought fiercely, even as part of him clamored for him to go on his knees and beg her forgiveness. To take her in his arms and hold her close, never letting go.

"But—" Tipper began.

"Hush." Diana's voice was subdued. "Mr. Byrne, it was no trouble. I was glad to be here."

She searched his eyes, and he forced himself to remember they had no future.

"Goodbye, Miss Smythe." He made her a precise bow, then pivoted and left the room before anyone could hear the sound of his heart breaking in two.

CHAPTER 33

THE TWO MONTHS ALLOTTED TO DEREK SPED PAST, AND before he knew it, all his farewells had been said. And if every night he dreamed of Diana Smythe's clear gray eyes, well, that was no one's business but his own.

Finally, the day of his departure came.

It felt odd to stride into the Southampton Spaceport as a ticketed passenger and not an officer of the law. Or a prisoner bound for transportation, thank all the bright stars.

He glanced up at the highest windows, lit with the morning sun, and remembered the view from up there: the intricate dance of spacecraft landing and taking off, the city of Southampton spreading to the River Itchen, and beyond.

Did Diana miss that view, or was she happy with her glittering life in London?

It didn't matter. He was leaving Earth, and Lady Diana Smythe, forever. The sorrow of it crouched on his shoulders, despite his efforts to shake the melancholy away.

He hefted his traveling valise and strode to berth 194, where the *Sláinte* waited to lift off. After much thought, he'd decided to take the last transport to New Eire. A brand new colony would be in need of policemen, and at least he had some experience in that regard, despite the bittersweet memories.

There was a small crowd gathered at the bay when he arrived—well-wishers saying their final farewells to friends and family. He didn't expect anyone to be there for him, but the sound of someone calling his name drew him up short.

"Derek! Oi, Derek Byrne!"

He turned, to see the small figure of Tipper waving wildly at him. Director Quinn stood just beyond, and next to him—Derek's heart squeezed tight in his chest—Diana.

He'd feared she would come. He'd desperately hoped she would, as well. Curse him for an utter fool.

Director Quinn strode up, smiling, Tipper and Diana right behind him.

"Couldn't let you go without saying goodbye," the director said. "I hear New Eire's a lovely planet."

"So they say." It wasn't home, of course. But it was rumored to be a green and lovely place, and Derek supposed he could do worse.

"Hope so." Tipper grinned at him. "Since we're going with you."

"What?" Derek blinked at the boy. Surely he hadn't heard the words aright.

Diana stepped forward. "We're going to New Eire, too."

The world tipped on its axis, and Derek simply stared at her. Were they playing an elaborate joke on him?

"But… what about London?" he asked.

"I left there two months ago," she said. "It wasn't the life for me."

The metal decking beneath his feet felt suddenly soft, malleable, as everything he thought was true shifted. If he weren't careful, he'd sink through to some entirely different reality.

"And your work at the spaceport?" He tried again to impose order on the world. To remind Diana of all the reasons she should remain on Earth.

"Alas, no." Director Quinn shook his head. "Much as I tried to entice Miss Smythe to return to work with me, she is set on a different course."

Diana sent the director a quick glance, the hint of a smile on her face. "You didn't try *that* hard, sir."

"We're going to start a school for pilots," Tipper said, bouncing up and down on his toes. "Director Quinn is helping, and Diana's fortune is providing the funding."

"On New Eire?" Derek felt as though his brain were filled with molasses, his thoughts syrupy and slow as he tried to follow the turn of events.

"Yes," Diana said. "Some of the best instructors in the galaxy will be teaching there—"

"Thanks to your money," Tipper cut in.

Diana ignored the interruption. "And in addition to the colonists, the school is open to any streetrat from Earth who wants to register. Passage paid."

"Though they must stay enrolled for at least a year," the director added, "or they'll be shipped home again with nothing to show for it."

"On New Eire?" Derek knew he was repeating himself,

but he could not quite grasp it. "And you'll be there, Diana? Tipper too?"

"Aye." Tipper showed his crooked-toothed smile again. "We're to be part of the first class of students, though Diana will show us all up, I'm thinking."

She ruffled the boy's hair fondly. "Don't sell yourself short, Tip. You're a clever one, you are."

Privately, Derek agreed with Tipper. Diana, with her brilliant mind, would quickly surpass the rest of the students. Before they knew it, she'd be commanding the cockpit of a ship.

Then he shook himself, pulling his thoughts down from dreams of spaceships to focus on Diana once more.

"You're set on going to New Eire, and leaving Earth?" he asked. Once more, to be absolutely sure.

"Yes." She met his gaze, her gray eyes clear.

The past fell away, and he was suddenly lighter than air. Not even gravity itself could hold him.

He pulled in a deep breath, then another. The universe was offering him a fresh start, and he'd be an idiot not to seize it with everything he was worth.

"Please, Diana, forgive me," he said. "I know I was unkind—worse than unkind—when last we met. I pushed you away because, well, because I never thought you'd want this."

He gestured at the bulk of the passenger ship, the carts teetering with stacked luggage, the laughing, teary goodbyes.

"But I do want this." She gave him a steady look. "And I forgive you, Derek. I was hoping that, after all that's happened, we might still be friends."

She held out her hand. No gloves, he noted. Lady Diana Smythe was gone for good.

Slowly, his heart banging in his chest, he took her hand. Their palms touched, warmth to warmth, and the world thumped back onto a steady axis.

"All aboard!" The announcement rang through the bay. "All aboard for passage to New Eire."

He still didn't quite believe it, but there was Diana, holding his hand, Tipper grinning at them. The hatch of the *Sláinte* stood wide, ready to welcome passengers destined for a new world.

Sometimes, no matter the burdens of the past, the only course was to go forward. To follow the compass of one's heart, straight into the stars.

The End

Ready for more stories set in the Victoria Eternal universe? Grab a copy of <u>Stars & Steam</u>, and read the short story that inspired *Star Compass!* www.antheasharp.com

Join Anthea's <u>newsletter</u> and get a bonus **free** story – plus find out more about her *USA Today* bestselling books, new releases and sales~ http://www. subscribepage.com/AntheaSharp